MW00942792

LARA
OF THE
NORTH

A. R. HENRICKSON

All rights reserved. No part of this book may be reproduced,
scanned, or distributed in any printed or electronic form
without permission of the author.

Copyright ©2019 A.R. Henrickson

Map by FreeVectorMaps.com

ISBN 978-0-359-61015-0

Henrik Johannes Fossum was confirmed at Gjerpen Kirke on the same day as his childhood playmate, playwright Henrik Ibsen. Ibsen came from a wealthy family, but Henrik Johannes came from a line of poor tenant farmers and metal workers. Henrik Johannes extracted bog iron at the Fossum Ironworks, located between Bo and Skien, Norway until 1849 when he left Norway and settled in Oceana County, Michigan. In America, he went by Henrik Henrickson, or Big Henry. I dedicate this book to Big Henry—my great-grandpa

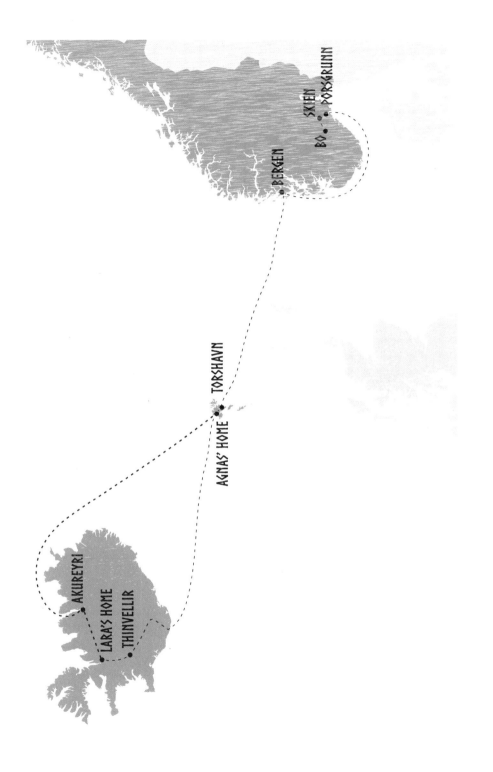

AKUREYRI

LARA'S HOME
THINVELLIR

AGNAS' HOME
TORSHAVN

BERGEN

BØ
SKIEN
PORSGRUNN

CHAPTER 1
NORTHERN ICELAND

One night during Skammdegi, the dark winter days, I climbed into the loft above the hearth and fell like a stone onto my pallet. I had worked hard all day in our cold sod house, feeding the fire, cooking the mutton stew, washing, sweeping, and keeping my little brother Ole from losing life and limb just by being a busy, curious toddler. Now he slept like an angel in the cradle near the hearth. I knew Modir was tired, too, but she kept the fire stoked while waiting for Fadir to return from an evening at the longhouse. I woke with a start when the door slammed against the fierce winter wind and Fadir stomped the snow off his boots. From my perch in the loft, I could eavesdrop unseen while Fadir reported the local news to Modir.

His chair creaked as he sat by the fire. "Old Harald was so drunk last week, he lost his right foot to frostbite after a long wander home. Young Gunnar asked for his extra boot so he would have a spare." Fadir chuckled.

"Stakkkars!" Modir exclaimed, "Poor Harald."

"Ja," agreed Fadir. "And the old shepherd woman, Fru Ashild, lost her hand."

"Ah! Also frostbite?" Modir asked.

"Nei. She was accused of stealing Fru Arnesen's gold earrings, though no one has found them among the hag's thing in the huddle by the pit house. Fru Arnesen says the stealing of her earrings was a 'crime of opportunity.' "

Modir clucked, "The Arnesens and their boys are high and mighty up on the hill in their fine yellow manor house. What do they know of suffering and mercy? So, Ashild's punishment was meted out here rather than waiting to send her to the Althing?"

I heard Fadir huff breath into his palms and rub his rough hands together, warming them. "Ah, ja. Fru Arnesen floated some dried meadowsweet in water and its shadow fell on Ashild."

Modir interrupted, "But dried Meadowsweet is not right; only fresh Meadowsweet can find out a thief."

Fadir continued, "Even so, Ashild was relieved of her hand by Herre Arnesen. A hatchet over a stump and -- off it dropped into the snow. Her shepherding work will be more difficult now, of course."

Modir replied, "Ack." She stirred the embers of the fire and kindling crackled. With my eyes closed, I imagined the sparks flying. Ole murmured in his cradle. Modir continued, "Sure, life was hard when the sawmills closed in Trondhjem, but I wonder if we should have stayed in Norway by our families, after all."

"Ah, well." I smelled the aroma of Fadir's pipe and the clunk, clunk, clunk as Modir churned butter. Fadir said, "I like to live by the old Viking saying, 'A man should be happy and in good humor to his dying day.'" His chair creaked when he rocked it back as was his habit. "And you know, metal work did not suit me. I am a farmer at heart."

Modir did not speak, but I imagined the expression on her face while she was thinking of how much she missed her family and homeland.

Glad to be snug in my bed, I rolled over and pulled my blanket up over my shoulders. I shivered at the thought of the drunk's foot and hag's hand in the ice pile waiting with the departed for spring burial. And after spring, would come summer. Finally it would be my turn to go to the annual Althing meeting at Thingvellir. I would be allowed to leave the estate to go and hear the memorized laws proclaimed from the Parliamentary Law Rock by the Law Speaker. Everyone knew that at Althing, the Logretta Chieftains determined just punishments for those accused of crimes, like theft and murder. And although justice for major crimes was the stated purpose of the Parliamentary Althing, for the young men and maids who attended, it was the social event of not only the year, but perhaps of a lifetime. This year, three maids from the Arnesen estate would go: Edda, Kristin, and me. Edda, an orphan, worked in the Arnesen's kitchen, and Kristin's fadir was a shareholding farmer, like my Fadir. Thoughts of the trip and our preparations filled my head as I tried to go back to sleep.

During the cold months, I rushed through my daily chores, because preparing for the journey and festival was at least half the excitement of the trip. We maids spent late afternoons in the pit house sewing shifts and tunics from cloth that was left over from the more costly pieces reserved to sell to merchants. We wove colorful belts from dyed scraps on small hand-held looms amid side-eyed glances from younger maids and indulgent smiles from older women who remembered their time at Thingvellir. After choosing which new belt each of us would wear on our trip, we would trade the extras at Althing market.

Edda took hold of the belt I was working on, "Lara, this is so much prettier than mine."

Kristin teased, "It's sturdy, too. You will be able to carry a lot of heavy wife keys." Maids at Thingvellir were often courted and found husbands there. On their wedding day, husbands hand over the keys to all they own to their wives in a gesture of trust and generosity.

"Oh, to be the receiver of such pure devotion!" Edda looked heavenward with her hands clasped over her heart. Kristin giggled.

"I could hold a four-leaf clover over a keyhole and blow on it instead," I said.

Kristin said, "Ja, that would open a lock, too, if you could find a lucky clover."

"Girls! Keep your mind on your work!" admonished the pit house matron. "Lara, sing a lovely tune that we may spin and weave in peace."

I paused, deciding not to sing any of the bawdy drinking songs I knew from Fadir's late-night sessions at the longhouse. Nor did I think the matron would be pleased with the pagan tunes I learned from the old shepherd women in the summer hills. What had I sung the last time she asked? My mind was a blank. Kristin's eyes met mine and I shrugged.

Kristin piped up, "I will sing a good Christian hymn with a lovely tune." She cleared her throat and began in a soft, clear voice:

Ah, holy Jesus, how hast thou offended,
that we to judge thee have in hate pretended?
By foes derided, by thine own rejected,
O most afflicted!
Lo, the Good Shepherd for the sheep is offered;
the slave hath sinned, and the Son hath suffered.
For our atonement, while we nothing heeded,
God interceded.

After Kristin sang the final note, there was a silent pause. Sweet, pious Kristin. Her voice was as pure and clear as a church bell ringing high on a hill.

With a sudden thought, I interrupted the quiet, "That song about sheep reminds me: do any of you know who we must ask about sheep to take with us to the Althing? Maybe the master?"

The matron shook her head, "Tisk, tisk."

Maud, one of the older maids spoke, "Not the master. The tall twin, Pjetur, is the one to ask. His fadir has given him oversight of some of the livestock." A wave of groans and a few nervous giggles filled the room. Maud continued, "I am sure you have heard what he did at the last long-house dance."

We all leaned forward, setting our weaving in our laps. "Tell us!"

Maud took a big breath. "Everyone knows that Pjetur is known to stick his big nose where it does not belong, including under maids' skirts. Well, he grabbed a maid and as he pulled her outside, he ripped her shift. Her fadir went after Pjetur. What a commotion. Then some other maids at the longhouse that night told that Pjetur had pinched and grabbed them, too. So now the fadirs have banned Pjetur from the longhouse."

A chorus of feminine voices chimed in: "Oooooh," "I heard that, too," "I saw it; I was there," "He scares me." Dismayed heads wagged from side to side and bent again to spinning and weaving.

"Something happened with Pjetur at the farm shed, too," I said. Weaving halted once again and all eyes turned to me. "One afternoon, Modir went into the animals' shed, and I heard her scream. Fadir came running from the orchard and I ran from the house, just in time to see Pjetur with his pants down around his knees, stumbling out the other end of the shed. Modir said Pjetur was doing something unspeakable to a ewe." Gasps echoed in the pit house.

"An abomination before God!" proclaimed Kristin.

"Yes, indeed," said the matron, scowling. She quickly wound yarn around her spindle and dropped it in the basket by her stool. "We are done for today. Go home to your supper."

We gathered our things, strapped on our barrel–stave snow skis and wrapped warm woolen shawls over our heads and shoulders. Making our way along the snow-packed path, I said, "I do not want a husband like the Arnesen twins." Little puffs of breath hung in the air as I spoke.

Kristin agreed, "Ja. Lads like that are evil."

Edda said, "But rich. They could provide a comfortable life for a maid."

Kristin scowled a bit and then brightened, "Lara! When we return from our trip, could you teach me how to make waterproof cloth like your Modir's cape?"

Edda said, "If I knew how to make it, I could sell it and get anything I want."

I couldn't think of anything I might want more than the adventure of Thingvellir. "It will be a while before I can teach you. We will be away for nearly a month."

Tying her shawl against the wind, Kristin said, "Ja! A week to get to the Althing, a week there, and another week to return. It will be a long, hard walk." I was undaunted by the prospect of the long trip; I was used to hiking all day -- either in the hills herding sheep, chasing young Ole, or walking for hours back and forth at the large loom, weaving weft through warp. And thinking of the temperate mid-summer weather was appealing on this damp, cold evening.

"The return trip may take longer than a week. Our eagerness to return to work may not equal our excitement to be away." I reasoned.

"But if I engage a rich suitor, my future will be something to look forward to," said Edda. "I wonder which of the lads from the estate will accompany us?" She rubbed her arms against the cold wind.

I sighed. Most maids were like Edda, hoping to meet a husband at the Althing. Love might be nice, but I wanted freedom and adventure more than anything. And I certainly did not want to marry a scoundrel like the Arnesen lads. I shook my head; my mind returned to practical things. "We have to ask Pjetur about the sheep."

"I do not want to do it," said Kristin. She dramatically held her palms out as if pushing against a wall.

Nearing the animal shed, I reached down and picked up two pieces of straw. "Short straw talks to Pjetur." I kept one straw whole and broke the other one into two unequal pieces. Then, turning away, I hid the ends in my hand. As I turned to face them, I said, "Both of you pick at once and I will take what is left."

Kristin and Edda looked skeptically at the straws. Kristin began to reach out and Edda quickly snatched a straw. Kristin grabbed another. I slowly opened my hand to reveal the short straw.

CHAPTER 2

I procrastinated. Soon, newborn lambs, marsh marigolds, and sprouting garden plants signaled the approach of summer. I had put off the task of talking to Pjetur long enough. Early one sunny morning, I saw my opportunity. Pjetur was in the garden we tended, helping himself to new root vegetables. I was glad that he didn't make Modir pull them for him. Usually, when he came down to the garden or barnyard, he spoke to Modir and Fadir as if they were stupid or deaf, shouting and sometimes cursing. I hoped he was in a charitable mood and safe to approach.

With Ole on my hip, I circled around the garden so Pjetur could see me approaching. I didn't want to startle him and risk his anger. He shielded his pale watery eyes with his hand and squinted in the sunlight. "Who is it?" he growled as he stood to his full height. He looked like a slim, leafless birch topped with white cotton grass. I stopped near the edge.

"Excuse me. It is I, Lara, coming to ask you a question."

"Then ask it and get away." He shooed me with his pale, grimy hand.

"We – the other maids and I – are wondering about sheep from the Master to take with us to Thingvellir."

Pjetur looked at me with his squinty eyes, slowly brushed soil from the small potato in his hand, took a bite, and chewed with his mouth open.

He took his time as he looked beyond his long nose to survey me up and down. Then he laughed. "You have to be fifteen years to go. A skinny maid like you cannot be that old. I could throw you like a spear and hit that door." He swept his arm dramatically and pointed to the chicken shed an arrow shot away. I shifted Ole to my other hip while I contemplated my reply. I resisted the urge to point out that he was skinny, too. Pjetur continued, "Which other maids are going?"

"Kristin and Edda."

Pjetur bit his lower lip. "Is Edda the kitchen maid with haunches like a heifer? And Kristin the one with freckles and copper hair?" His puckered mouth made a loud smacking sound. "They both look ripe for the picking." I looked anxiously toward our turf hut, then used my apron to wipe Ole's nose. "I believe you maids will be needing company on your journey. My brodir Einar and I will go, too. And we will bring the sheep."

Einar, the short, stocky brother, was a vicious hunter. He was known to always wear a red hat over his unruly black hair. He was just as distasteful as his tall twin, but in a different way. In pit house gossip, I heard that he once found a lamb that had strayed from another farm. Instead of returning it to its owner, he tied a rope from his horse to the back legs of the poor creature and dragged it bleating through a boiling geyser stream. As the animal suffered and died, Einar rode on, whistling and waving his red hat in the air. So learning that the twins would join us on our journey made my spirit sink like a ship in a deep swell. "Thank you," I said and I bowed slightly as I backed out to the garden's edge, my distrustful eyes on Pjetur. After I turned to hurry to our hut, I glanced back and saw that he followed me with his piggy eyes. Edda and Kristin would not be any happier than I was about Einar and Pjetur joining our traveling group. I tumbled the conversation in my mind, wondering if I could have said or done something to discourage the twins from joining us.

Carrying a wash bucket, Modir came around the front of our hut as I approached. "Ole," she said to the child in my arms, "A big two-year-old lad does not need to be carried everywhere. Now go on inside." I put Ole down and watched him toddle past a chicken to the door. Modir turned to me. "Lara, what was that then? I saw you talking to Pjetur."

The words tumbled out as I explained about the short straw, the sheep, and Pjetur's unexpected and disturbing response. "Modir, the maids will be afraid to go now. I am, too. We don't like the twins." I chewed my thumbnail.

"I'll talk to your fadir about it." Modir went in the hut, "Ole, get your hand out of the butter churn. Uff da. Lara! Come get your brodir."

CHAPTER 3

That night, after asking God's blessing on our supper of mutton stew, Fadir announced, "Dottir, tonight we start some new lessons for you."

Modir said, "I will wash up and put Ole to bed."

I wondered if Modir told Fadir about the Arnesen twins going along to Thingvellir. I was curious, but knew Fadir well enough to trust that he would explain when he was ready. I ate quickly, but Fadir took his time. I waited while he slowly scraped the last of the stew from his bowl and wiped his face with his kerchief. He looked across the table as me and winked, then stood and motioned for me to follow him to the high shelf where he kept his tools out of Ole's reach. With his back to me, Fadir picked up something and held it where I could not see, turning to face me with his hands behind his back. "Pick one," he said. I considered, then tapped his left arm. Smiling, he swung his arm around and opened his hand. Nothing. Then he swung his right arm around. His hand held his well-worn sling fashioned from smooth wood and supple leather. He held it out to me. "This was mine when I was a boy in Norway. Now it is yours." He looked at me from under his bushy eyebrows and smiled. I took the sling and felt the warmth of Fadir's hand in the wood. It seemed like a holy relic. I thought about the custom that a fadir would usually save his things for his son, and I determined right then that I would pass it along to Ole someday.

"I will treasure it," I said.

"Ack! You will use it! Come. I will teach you."

Taking advantage of the evening sunlight, Fadir took me out behind our hut. "Look for stones like this." He rolled one around in his fingers. "They will hit their marks with speed and accuracy." I found some stones that met with his approval and put them all in my apron pocket. Fadir produced a sack of last-year's moldy potatoes and together we lined a few up on the garden fence. Fadir then stood near our hut's door, took the sling, swung it, and deftly sent a potato flying into the next field. He moved me closer to the fence and handed me the sling. My first attempt fell far short. Then, the fence and nearby shrubs took a beating, but the potatoes remained entirely still and unmarked. They had a better chance of rotting and dropping off the fence on their own than being knocked off by my shots. Fadir patiently watched and adjusted my arms without saying much.

Each night I improved and Fadir moved me farther away from my targets. The week progressed, and I finally I succeeded in not only pummeling potatoes but even graduated to exploding small clods of dirt from an arrow shot's distance away. Fadir's eyes shone. "Dottir, you have an eagle eye and a steady hand." As we refilled my pockets with stones, Fadir said, "Do you remember the Bible story of David and Goliath? The giant Goliath was defeated by a shot to the temple. It's a vulnerable spot on any man." Fadir kicked the dirt with the toe of his worn boot to loosen a stone and continued, "Another spot lower down would slow a man either with a shot from the sling or a well-placed knee." He looked at me and I thought I saw the edges of his mouth turn up a bit. Fadir then motioned for me to follow him back to our hut. He cleared his throat. "Traveling can be dangerous. There may be scoundrels and outlaws in the barren places. I have thought to ask you not to go to the Althing, but I know how much this trip means to you. I asked Herre Arnesen if I could accompany you and the other maids. He said that with the twins going, he cannot spare me. But," he paused and looked toward heaven, "I've learned that Tryggve Elvarsson, his cousin Olav, and another trustworthy lad from the Andersson's farm are going, so I've arranged for you to all travel together in a group. And Herre Arnesen has a horse to be delivered to a farm south of here, so he said I could hitch it to the wagon along with Old Red and give you young folks a ride part way. After I deliver the horse, Old Red and I will take the wagon back home. Then you and the others will be on your own. Just stay with the group."

"Safety in numbers," I said, "just like the sheep,"

As he turned toward the barn, Fadir mumbled, "Sheep among wolves."

CHAPTER 4

Spring turned to summer and finally it was time for our much-awaited journey. On the day before our departure, I rushed through my chores to finish packing. I shook the rugs, saw the sand fly away and thought, Soon that will be me, flying away! Ole fussed and held my legs as I tried to work. "Do not worry, Ole," I said. "I will come back before you know it and I will bring you a special treat from the market." Ole's gray eyes looked doubtful.

I planned to travel in my old clothes, so I carefully folded and packed my new shift and apron to wear once we got to Thingvellir. These are the other things I packed: my new belt and bonnet, the bone hair comb Modir says came from Bestemor in Norway, my wooden bowl, Modir's water-proof cape, and extra woven belts to trade at the Thingvellir market.

Breathless, Kristin arrived at the door that evening. "Lara! Did you pack your slingshot?"

"Right here." I patted my pocket.

Kristin prattled on, "I have flint for making fire and an old piece of sailcloth we can share for shelter. The preacher gave me a Bible to bring along. Edda has sturdy twine. And one of the stable hands made a map of our journey on her old apron. I think we are ready."

"So, we leave at daybreak," I replied. I could feel the excitement building in my belly and I wondered if I would sleep at all that night.

Kristin leaned in and gave me a quick hug. "I will see you in the morning. You know, Lara, when we return, we will be different. Our journey will make us women."

I pondered Kristin's words. Maybe she was right: I may no longer feel like a girl when I return. Modir told me I became a woman when my new moon bleeding began during the last of the cold dark days. She gave me my own cloth strips to keep clean and now I put them in my pack as well. I did not feel like a woman with the bleeding; I only felt irritated and bothered. But this journey will be a true adventure that could set my life on a whole new course. I looked around the hut to memorize everything. No doubt, I will see my home with new eyes after the journey.

After a fitful night, I rose before the sun, quickly dressed, and laced my boots that Fadir re-soled and polished for my trip. I bent down to carefully slide my small blade in the side of my boot, then straightened to see Modir sleepily light the fire to warm the breakfast porridge. For the last time in a while, I did my daily chore of emptying the chamber pots into the urine barrel. Fadir shuffled over to the worn table to join us. Ole stirred in his cradle. He is growing. When I return, he will be even taller and will soon need a bigger bed. Ole sat up, rubbed his eyes, held out his arms, and said my name, "Wawa."

I picked him up and gave him a kiss. "Say Lara."

"Wawa."

"By the time I return, he may be able to say his Ls and Rs," I thought aloud. Modir and Fadur ate in silence with their heads down. I had witnessed Ole learning to crawl, walk, and learn words, and I felt a bit sad that I might miss other milestones while away. I changed his diaper, and brought him to the table, lingering longer than usual while holding him close and inhaling the scent of his hair. He pointed to his porridge and I said, "Mmmmmm."

"Mmmmm," he repeated in his sweet baby voice.

Fadir rose from the bench, "I will ready the horses and wagon." I watched his silhouette approach the doorway, his back stooped. I had not thought of him as old until that moment.

I ate my porridge in a hurry, washed my bowl, and tucked it in my pack. A sliver of sunlight peeking from behind the mountain glinted through the window. Gravel crunched and I heard voices outside. "Lara!" Edda called. "Come on." I grabbed my pack, hugged Modir, and kissed Ole's fair head.

Modir held my arm, and took a small package from her apron pocket. She pressed the package into my hand. "For you," she whispered. "Open it later. When you are alone."

I squeezed Modir's hand and quickly tucked the package in my pocket. Sunlight caught a tear on her cheek. Seeing Modir's sadness made my eyes well. I did not want to cry in front of the others, so I quickly turned, blinked fast, and went outside to the group waiting for me. Behind Kristin and Edda, the tall, fair, broad-shouldered cousins Tryggve and Olav first caught my eye, and then I also spotted their smaller, dark-haired friend Birgir. I knew all of them from church. A quick bark made me look down, "Who is this?" I bent and scratched under the chin of a shaggy black dog.

Tryggve replied, "That's Raven, the best sheep dog around. He's going with us." Raven's tail wagged and his face formed a smile.

Fadir approached with the wagon and we clambered in. It was already a bit of a tight squeeze, and then Raven jumped in. We all reached for him, but he chose to sit with Tryggve. I looked at the gathered faces. "Where are the twins? They are supposed to bring the sheep."

"They were not at the agreed-upon meeting place this morning. I say we go on without them." Olav said. The others nodded their agreement.

Not having the twins along might make the trip more enjoyable, but without the sheep, we would not have much to trade at the market. I shrugged. We would still have an adventure. I turned to see Modir hold Ole who struggled to join us. I waved farewell. Fadir clucked and lifted the reins, the wagon jolted, and we were on our way.

CHAPTER 5
JOURNEY TO THINGVELLIR ICELAND

Following the rutted path, Fadir drove the wagon southward. He joined in when we sang old songs loudly and out of tune. We waved to farmers in their fields as we passed until the farms grew few and far between. The sun rose higher and Raven's fur felt like a warm mitten. We covered a lot of ground before we stopped mid-day to deliver Herre Arnesen's horse to the waiting farmer. "Eh there!" Fadir called to the man at the end of a long driveway. "Are you hoping for a horse today?" The farmer waved his hat in reply. Fadir turned to our group and said, "Now it is time for us to part." We climbed out of the wagon and Fadir also climbed down. Not one to show affection, I was surprised when he drew me close. He whispered in my ear, "Take care of yourself." I nodded and he turned, hoisted himself back in the wagon seat, and called to us, "Follow your map and the stone path markers, and you will find your way." Then he waved and I watched him go down the long drive to where the farmer was waiting.

"We should walk until we are tired and then stop for a meal. The wagon ride gave us a good head start," Tryggve said.

Full of energy, Raven bounded ahead and we followed. Along the way, we picked wildflowers and fashioned crowns for our heads. We laughed and bowed and curtseyed to each other but kept up our pace. After a while, Edda consulted her apron map and we saw that we were at the end of our home fjord. The water ran in a stream and then dwindled to a trickle. Just as we had been told, stone cairns began to appear along the path, confirming our route. We followed the cairns until we were weary, and then stopped.

When we had set out the food and gathered to eat, in his quiet voice, Birgir said he had something to show us. From his pack, he pulled a wooden stave with an inscription on it: If this sign is carried, one will never lose one's way in storms or bad weather, even when the way is not known. "It is a Vegvisir. My Fadir's fadir made it for us. He said he made one for my fadir when he went to Thingvellir, also, and he did not lose his way." Birgir frowned. "I guess the stave got lost, though, because Afi had to make a new one for me." We laughed. Birgir passed around the stick for us to admire before he carefully returned it to his pack.

"I am starving!" Olav declared. He took a big bite of cheese and showed us his happy full mouth when we heard something approaching. Tryggve, Olav, and Birgir jumped to their feet with knives drawn. I held my sling. Looking toward the sound, I first saw a bright red hat cresting a nearby hill and then another head with white flyaway hair: Einar and Pjetur. True to Pjetur's word, they each had sheep tethered to their saddles. We all relaxed a bit seeing the familiar faces, but I cannot say I was happy to see them. Even with the provision of sheep, the addition of the twins to our group felt like a dark cloud before a storm. Edda, acting the hostess, invited the twins to share our food. The twins surprised us all by offering to share the water and beer they had brought. I watched them warily, but they sat with the boys and gave us maids only passing glances. After we ate, Edda spread out her apron map so we could again be sure that we were on the right path. Einar pointed to the spot where he thought we were, and his dirty finger left a brown smudge on the apron. Uff da!

Before we resumed our journey, I found a private place to relieve myself behind a rock. When I finished, I sat on the rock and took out the package Modir had given me. Folded carefully inside a note was a silver pendant on a woven silver chain. Such a fine piece of jewelry may attract avarice and trouble, so I put the necklace over my head and tucked it inside my bodice. The note from Modir said, "This was made by my brodir, your Norwegian Fraendi Tollaf Henriksen, the solvsmed from Skien. Ole will receive one like it some day. I bless you and your trip with this gift." I had studied my letters and numbers with Modir and Fadir all these years, but had never received a note from them until now. I carefully folded it and put it in my pocket before making my way back to the group. But for the rest of that evening my thoughts stayed on Modir's words, her gift, and her family in Norway. I wondered if I would ever know them.

CHAPTER 6

Rested and fed, we continued on our way. Tryggve untied the sheep from the twins' saddles so Raven could do his herding job. The dog expertly kept the sheep near the path, bringing up the rear of our little parade. When evening approached, Einar took off on his horse across a field toward a patch of shrubbery. When he caught up with us, he was holding high in the air two large hares. "Supper!" he called. Maybe having the twins along would prove helpful after all.

We set to work. Even away from the farm, there were chores to do: Olav started a fire while Kristin and I prepared a spit to turn the meat as it cooked. Tryggve and Birgir skinned the hares and hung the pelts to dry. Olav turned the horses and sheep out to graze. Pjetur and Einar drank beer and watched. Edda sat by the fire, rotating the hares on the spit. She removed her boots. "Oh!" she exclaimed. Her left heel had a large blister. Seeing her distress, I found a stone that had cooled in the shade and set it on her foot. "Bring me my pack?" she pointed to her brown bag. After rummaging around, she produced a small pouch. She took a piece of root from it. "For pain," she explained as she chewed thoughtfully on it, like a cow chewing its cud. Soon after we ate, she fell asleep with her pack as a pillow. I covered her with her shawl.

Lying near the sheep, Raven rested his head on his paws and his eyes met mine with what looked like an appeal. Of course! He had been working all day without food or water. Tryggve must have forgotten. I took my slingshot out in the midsummer evening light. Away from the fire, it was easy to spot scampering rodents crisscrossing the flat, rocky terrain. I took aim at one that paused a short distance away and the stone hit it squarely on the head. I waited patiently until another came sniffing the carrion and killed that one, too. I fetched the two by their tails and as I approached Raven, he stood to watch me, wagging his tail, his open mouth forming a smile. Once he began to tear into his feast, I got my bowl and filled it at the nearby stream, then brought it to the thirsty dog. "I believe we are going to be good friends," I said as I scratched behind his ears. He looked up at me and licked his chops.

When I rinsed out my bowl and went back to the fire, I sat by Tryggve and told him I had fed Raven. He startled, then hung his head. "I can't believe I forgot. Thank you."

Birgir, in his quiet voice, was telling old stories about elves and trolls whose antics and devilry made them appealing and scary both. "… and when she guessed the name of the old crone, the hag fell on the ground and disappeared into smoke." His story telling lulled us, and one by one, we slumped down onto our blankets and slept until morning.

When we woke, the fire was cold, but Edda's foot was hot and red. Kristin looked at it and frowned, "My Fraendi Ivan had a sore like this on his foot. Remember him? He's the one with a missing leg. They had to take it off to save his life!"

Edda shook and tears flooded her eyes. "I don't want to lose my leg! Or die!" She gingerly put her sock and boot back on when it was time to resume our journey. Kristin and I held her arms to lessen the pressure as she walked, but it was clear that we could not make it the rest of the long trip this way.

"Sure would be neighborly to let Edda ride on a horse!" I hinted loudly.

After our mid-day stop, Pjetur said, "I suppose she can ride with me if she has to. She is making us go too slow." I had hoped he would walk and let Edda ride the horse alone, but she quickly climbed up and sat astride the horse with Pjetur behind her. I thought the arrangement was unseemly but knew that an injury like Edda's could be serious. So I resolved to be grateful to Pjetur for sharing his ride. Even so, Kristin and I linked arms and walked behind them to keep an eye on the sheep -- and Pjetur. Before evening, his arm holding the reins grazed Edda's breast and his other hand rested on her thigh. Edda had a slight smile on her face but otherwise seemed not to notice.

I whispered to Kristin, "Do you see what I see? Is Edda inviting his advances?" Kristin scowled and shrugged.

After our foraged supper of birds' eggs and wild berries, I asked Edda and Kristin to accompany me to relieve ourselves. Once out of earshot of the boys, Kristin and I began to talk in urgent whispers to Edda. "Are you letting Pjetur take advantage of you? You should tell him to keep his hands to himself. Are you not afraid of what else he might do?"

Edda smiled placidly, "I can take care of myself; you fret too much." Even so, Kristin and I huddled close to Edda at the fire to sleep that night and I tucked my small blade in my bodice where it made a comforting clink against my silver pendant.

CHAPTER 7

In the morning, I sensed rustling of the others as they wakened and I shivered. Overnight, the weather had turned cool, damp, and windy. No sunshine to brighten our path today! After a big breakfast, we agreed not to stop mid-day, moving quickly instead to stay warm and cover ground. Much like sitting in our familiar family church pews, we had fallen into a regular order as we traveled. Einar, with his red hat, was the trailblazer, easy to spot high on his horse, even if he got ahead of us. Next walked the three boys, Tryggve, Olav, and Birgir. Then came Edda and Pjetur on his horse, wrapped in a single blanket. Kristin and I followed with Raven and the sheep, plodding along and trying to keep warm, our shawl-covered heads down. We safely crossed a bog bean marsh where the roots formed a dense carpet. We avoided cotton grass marshes where the roots were poor and sinking was likely.

I heard Edda giggle and glanced up to catch Pjetur resting his chin on her shoulder. Ack! She was asking for trouble. Then Edda held the reins, so Pjetur's hands were free to roam under the blanket that covered them both. I fumed and huffed as we hustled along. Surely, Edda knew Pjetur's bad reputation. She would not get a good husband and be able to be married in the church if Pjetur steals her virginity. And what were the chances that a wealthy landowner's son would marry a lowly kitchen orphan? Edda should be more prudent and make Pjetur know that his advances were unwelcome.

After a full day of being cold and irritated, I was ready for a warm fire, food, and some rest when evening finally arrived. Thank God, Olav thought to put dry kindling in his pack. Kristin's flint and Olav's kindling had just gotten the fire blazing when the skies that had threatened all day rumbled. First, small drops sizzled the fire, but then rain put it out entirely as if by a bucket. Kristin quickly unfolded her sailcloth and we huddled under it as we ran to a nearby outcropping of rocks. There the eight of us squeezed in and held the sailcloth. Squinting when lightning flashed, I could just make out the outlines of the horses and sheep. Tethered to bushes, the horses hung their heads as the wind and rain pelted their backsides. Raven huddled by the sheep, head down but eyes watchful.

Joining with the bleating sheep, Olav began the complaints, "I am so hungry, I could eat a horse."

Tryggve said, "I am so hungry, I could eat a whale."

Kristin laughed and said, "I am so hungry, I could eat a plate of lutefisk." We all laughed; only the old folk liked the salted fish soaked in lye.

Birgir then began telling a fish story in his quiet voice. "Each time the old man pulled up his line, he found that he had snagged a boot, a sock, a hat, but no fish. Then he tried again…."

Soon, I heard Einar snoring at the far end of the huddle. I must have dozed off, too, because I was startled awake to realize the rain had stopped and then I heard whispers. I shifted my weight and saw Edda and Pjetur in the dim light. They were kissing! I jumped up, hitting my head on the rock above us. "What are you doing?" I yelled.

"Who? What?" The others tried to form words as they woke up.

"Pjetur. And Edda." I stuttered.

Pjetur looked at me calmly and said, "What do you mean? You woke me with your shouting. Edda, you were sleeping too, right?"

Edda glanced at me and then looked down. "Ja. Sleeping."

Pjetur continued, "I do not know what you think was happening; you must have been dreaming." He leaned forward, winked at the other boys and shrugged, "Girls."

CHAPTER 8

When daylight arrived, I asked Edda to remove her boot and sock so I could examine her foot. The spot was less red, but had broken open and was oozing clear fluid and a little watery blood. "Does it still hurt?" I asked.

"Oh, ja. I will chew some root today as I ride with Pjetur."

"Are you sure you cannot walk? Let me switch your socks so you'll have a cleaner, dryer one on your sore foot." I began to loosen her other boot.

Edda frowned. "Even if we make it more dry, I still will not be able to walk on it. Pjetur says I can ride with him the rest of the way."

Now it was my turn to frown, "Edda, are you sure you are safe with him? I am afraid for you."

"He is really not so bad, Lara. He tells me little jokes and lets me hold the reins. I think we should give him a chance."

"By we, do you mean that you want to give him a chance? With you?"

Edda finished tying her laces, stood up, and turned as she limped away, "Are you ready to go?" I silently fumed that she ignored my questions. While the group prepared to leave, the lads offered to bring up the rear with the sheep. Faithful dog Raven kept the sheep in line while the boys horsed around with sticks and rocks. They were acting like unruly goats, laughing and jumping.

Not to be left out, Einar offered his horse to Edda so that he could join the lads and add his mischief to the mix.

"She is fine where she is," answered Pjetur gruffly. "If you do not want to ride, let someone else take your reins." Edda said nothing, but looked up at the sky as if she were studying an interesting bird.

Kristin and I jumped at the chance to ride and take the lead on Einar's horse. I helped Kristin up and then hoisted myself up and took the reins. I had not been astride a wide and muscular Islandic horse before. "I feel like I can see forever from up here," I said, looking over the sprawling vista of scrubby hills, gray rocks, and rivulets of steaming water.

A short distance away, I spotted a fox chasing a hare. Before the fox could catch it, I took aim with my slingshot and the hare jumped, then fell. "Nice shot!" Kristin exclaimed as I veered the horse toward the kill.

I was about to dismount when Einar ran up behind us and snatched the hare. "Put your sling away, Maid," he shouted. "I am the hunter." I rolled my eyes and watched him tether the hare to the back of Pjetur's pack.

Ahead on the path, a colorful tent caught my eye. As we approached, I saw that two men with provisions were camped there. "Join us," the man in a blue tunic called.

One by one, we gathered by the tent where food was laid out on a makeshift table. "You are traveling to Thingvellir?" he asked.

We all looked at one another, unsure if we should talk to the man, but then Pjetur sauntered up to him and spoke, "Who are you and why do you ask?"

"Ah, prudent young people!" he exclaimed. "No doubt you were warned about talking to strangers in the barren lands. But we are harmless traders, here to make your journey more pleasant." He waved his hand over the food. "If you have something to trade, or coins, we can give you some of this." We moved closer and looked at the spread, but Tryggve and Olav hung back, warily watching the strangers.

Olav spoke. "We have our own provisions and are on a schedule. We must keep going."

The other man stepped from behind the tent and Tryggve drew his knife. "Oh, that's not necessary." The smiling blue-tunic man held up his hands. "We mean you no harm; you may go in peace with our blessing."

Edda was the last to leave the table, looking back longingly at the food. But then she skipped to Pjetur's horse and he pulled her up. "We will be on our way, then," Pjetur proclaimed in a deep voice. Kristin and I climbed back on Einar's horse, and we continued on our way, but Tryggve and Olav walked backwards until the tent was out of view.

"Lara, do you think they meant us harm?" Kristin asked.

"I am not certain, but I had a bad feeling about them. I guess the lads did, too," I replied.

"Thank you, Jesus, for protecting our group." Kristin prayed with her eyes wide open. We passed hills and ravines that were marked on Edda's map and could see that we were getting closer to Thingvellir. Suddenly, Kristin began excitedly slapping my arm. "Look!" Kristin pointed, "The giant geyser!"

In the distance ahead, a plume of water as high as a mountain shot up to the sky. "I think it is the one on Edda's apron map!" I shouted as I felt my pulse quicken. "That means we are only a day away from Thingvellir!"

I turned to call back to the rest of the group. "Look! The geyser!"

The boys jumped and whooped and ran to a hill where they could see ahead. What a welcome sight. Einar raised his red hat high in the air. "Great Geyser, I salute you!"

Tryggve yelled, "We made it!" He ran back, kissed our horse and playfully tugged my boot.

Even the usually quiet Birgir shouted. "The Vegvisir worked! We did not get lost!"

Excited to reach our destination, we picked up our pace. All except Edda and Pjetur. Their horse loped along at the rear with the sheep, seeming reluctant to continue. Tryggve called, "Pjetur! Is your horse all right? "

Pjetur growled, "She is fine. Mind your own business." I looked at Edda. She was leaning back on Pjetur in an intimate way with an odd smile on her face. Was the sleepy effect of chewing that root making her do that?

That night we set up camp near the geyser. My hips ached from riding astride the wide horse. "Kristin, do your hips hurt?" I asked.

"Yes, and my seat as well. I will be just as glad to walk again tomorrow. I do not know how Edda can stand it."

"She is a bit wider than we are," I observed. "Maybe it is easier for her. Pjetur once talked of her as 'the one with haunches like a heifer.'"

"Disgusting." Kristin wrinkled her nose.

While we were busy preparing the campsite, I glanced up and saw Pjetur's horse carrying Edda and Pjetur toward a nearby hill. I doubted that Pjetur wanted to be able to see the geyser better from the hill. He no doubt wanted to see something of Edda's better. When they continued until they were out of sight behind the hill, I motioned for Tryggve. "Pjetur and Edda are on the other side of that hill." I pointed. "I'm worried…."

Tryggve's brows dipped. "I will get Olav and we will go check. Birgir will stay with you and Kristin." Einar was prowling for prey nearby. Shading my eyes with one hand, I fingered the chain of my necklace with the other, watching Tryggve and Olav stride over the rocks and boiling rivulets. As they approached the hill, I saw Pjetur's returning silhouette, and then Edda, trailing behind on the horse. When Pjetur got to the spot where the other boys waited, Pjetur shouted angry words, then stalked back to camp.

I ran to Edda and took hold of the horse's bridle, "What happened? What were you thinking, going off with Pjetur alone?"

Edda's face was slightly flushed. "I do not want talk about it."

"Edda…."

"Please, Lara." When we got to camp, Edda took her pack to the relieving spot behind some bushes where I spied her stuffing something under a rock. She crawled to her blanket, took some root from her pack, and chewed it with her eyes closed. She would soon be asleep. I went and looked under the rock. As I suspected, there was Edda's undershift, stained with the blood of her virginity. My heart sank as I slowly put it back. Edda wanted to follow her own mind, just like baby Ole when he wanted his way. I sat on the blanket next to her and reached for her hand. She snatched it away and as she did, a pair of gold earrings fell on the ground.

CHAPTER 9

I gasped. Were those the gold earrings stolen from the Mistress? The ones the old woman lost her hand for stealing? "Edda, wake up. What are these?"

Edda rolled over and mumbled. "From Pjetur." I did not know what to think. Did Pjetur steal from his own modir? Did he know the hag lost her hand when accused of stealing them? Did he give them to Edda in exchange for her virginity? Edda's snores told me that I wouldn't get any more answers from her root-addled mind tonight.

I joined the others at the fire where we ate roasted hare along with dried fish and cheese left from our traveling provisions. Then Kristin brought out her Bible, "In gratitude for our safe trip," she said. She read to us from the Psalms. "Lord, you have been our dwelling place … before the mountains were born…You have set our iniquities before you, our secret sins in the light of your presence."

"Enough of that," snarled Pjetur. He took his blanket and pack over by the horses. There is nothing like Scripture to convict a guilty heart, at least that is what Fadir says.

After Pjetur left, Kristin continued reading, but my thoughts wandered. I was weary from the trip, but my concern for Edda and my excitement about arriving at the Althing the next day kept my mind swirling. Thankfully, the geyser provided constant comforting sounds and I finally fell asleep. When we woke, the sun was already shining steadily and Edda seemed herself again.

Wanting to arrive at Thingvellir looking our best, we took turns, girls then boys, bathing in a tepid spring made private with a makeshift wall using Kristin's sailcloth and Edda's twine. Then we changed from our dusty traveling clothes to our clean new festival clothes. When I leaned over to put on my clean stockings, the sun caught my silver pendant. Edda asked, "What is that, Lara? It is beautiful!"

I quickly tied my fancy embroidered bodice and tucked in the silver piece. "A gift from Modir."

"I just love things like that." Edda said. I thought, Yes, I know.

"Avarice is a sin," said Kristin.

"A lot of things are supposed to be sins," Edda shrugged as she gathered her pack.

Kristin tisked and tucked her copper curls into her bonnet.

I wondered if the boys actually bathed or if they just pretended to, because they were ready to go so quickly. Einar resumed the lead on his horse, a fresh red hat like a beacon drawing us to Thingvellir. Clean and refreshed, I relished the slight cool breeze and sunshine of the morning, glad that I would not arrive at the festival wind-blown or sweaty. I admired my clean new shift and apron tied with my new belt.

Kristin took my hand, leaned in and whispered, "I am worried about Edda. Is she sinning with Pjetur? He is not likely to marry a farm servant."

"I wonder about that, too."

Kristin shook her head, "Not good."

I was about to tell Kristin about the earrings and Edda's bloody and torn undershift, but just then we crested a hill and I saw a wide rock canyon ahead. I was dumb struck. It looked as if a giant had swung a mighty ax and split the world. Thingvellir! The place every Icelander talks about into their old age. Only a chieftain or landowner would see this more than once in their lifetime. My heart began to pound and in my excitment, I began to sweat on my clean new shift. Odin's Eye!

CHAPTER 10
THINGVELLIR ICELAND

Drawing closer, we saw colorful tents, sod and stone huts, and heard sounds of music and laughter. Surely, this was the most wonderful place in the world! As we approached the campsites, Pjetur proclaimed, "Fadir provided ten sheep, one for each of you to trade and two each for Einar and me. Ours are the large ones with twine around their necks. Do not touch our four sheep. Do what you will with the rest."

The six of us discussed our plan and traded a sheep for two small tents: one for the lads and one for the maids. There was room to graze the sheep between the tents where Raven would keep his watchful eye on them. A private latrine and shitting log were also provided for our use. Our campsite seemed like a castle to me, but Pjetur and Einar set off to negotiate for finer lodging.

"Olav and I will shear and slaughter one of the sheep for our food," Tryggve offered. "We can then trade the wool for other goods."

Birgir said, "I'll make a fire pit here." He pointed to a flat spot.

"I'll help you gather rocks for the hearth," Kristin offered.

Edda and I carried our packs into the tent. "Edda, how is your foot?" I asked.

"I think it is better and being in one place will give me a chance to rest it," she replied. I did not point out that riding on Pjetur's horse was also resting her foot. "I think clean, dry stockings are also helping." I remember offering that idea earlier and she refused it. "I am going to go exploring. Will you come with me?" As she spoke, she casually put on the gold earrings.

"You are wearing those?" I asked.

Edda put her hands on her hips, "You are wearing your silver necklace?"

I paused and looked at Edda's face. I thought I saw a slight smile there.

"A woman lost her hand because of those earrings," I said.

Edda tossed her head. "I did not accuse her and I did not steal the earrings. But maybe someone will want to steal your pendant."

"No one can see my necklace tucked into my bodice."

"Maybe I like to show that I have pretty things," she replied.

"Someone may rip them right off your ears."

Edda hooked her arm into mine. "That is why you are going with me. Come on. We will explore and then we can tell the others where to find everything here."

I felt a little guilty leaving the others to work, but not guilty enough to stay. I checked for my slingshot and blade in my apron pocket.

When we went outside, Birgir and Kristin quickly moved apart. Her cheeks were flushed as she adjusted a rock with her boot. Birgir whistled tunelessly, looking at the sky, hands in his pockets. "We will be back soon," I said.

"We are fine here," Kristin called.

Since Althing was a two-week affair and we arrived after the first week, the revelers were in full swing. We passed food booths with ale, fine pastries, cheeses, and pickled fish. Our mouths watered as we passed each one. "We will have roasted mutton when we get back to our camp. Remember that." I spoke to myself as much as to Edda.

"I want to see the goods I might trade for," Edda replied, marching along without any evidence of a limp. Soon we came upon jewelry booths with copper, tin, and even silver pieces fashioned into crosses, flowers, and animal shapes. There were pendants on knitted chains or leather straps, rings, brooches, bracelets, earrings, and hairpins. Some had colorful polished stones of red or blue. Edda picked up a bracelet, copper with a red stone, held it to her wrist, "Ooooh!"

"We are just looking now, right, Edda?" I reminded her. "We do not even have our belts with us to trade. We should see all the goods before we decide."

Edda slowly returned the bracelet to the vendor's table. The jeweler immediately polished it on his sleeve and put it in a different spot on the table. "For those with means," he growled. Edda tossed her head in reply and the dangling gold earrings caught the man's admiring eyes. "Come back and buy," he said as he caressed the bracelet with a smile.

Beeswax and honey were at the next table. A monk was bartering for wax candles. "How many coins for these?" he asked, then added, "For the church." I was astounded to hear how much the wax was worth and noted to myself that I should pursue beekeeping in the future. Perhaps a beeskep in modir's garden.

We had already been away from our campsite for too long, so we quickly passed by the ironworkers with grave crosses and cooking pots as well as the wood workers with buckets, churns, and tableware. The craftsmen called out offers to landowners and chieftains to build furniture and even houses or ships.

When we returned to our campsite, we had only seen a small portion of the market and none of the law-keeping places or the entertainment tents. My eagerness to come here was not unfounded; this would be a most exciting week!

CHAPTER 11

I saw the smoke of the cooking fire as we approached our campsite and smelled the mutton roasting. Tryggve and Olav were leaning on some rocks, sipping from their drinking horns. "What do you have there?" I asked.

"Birgir and Kristin went to an ale booth and brought some back for us."

"Kristin, did you use one of your belts in trade?" I asked, hoping she wasn't spending them on the lads.

"No, they traded some of the wool they just sheared. And Birgir brought some things to trade." At that, Birgir brought out a roll of wool tied with twine. He unrolled it on the ground and revealed its contents: bone pieces carved into toys, flutes, needles, and figures of animals. "Isn't he talented?" Kristin beamed. "He says he likes to carve while he tells stories in the evening to entertain his family or the men in the longhouse." Birgir's face and neck turned red and he looked sheepishly at Tryggve and Olav who snickered behind their ale horns.

Tryggve straightened and said, "Olav and I brought things to trade as well." Olav disappeared into their tent and returned with two rolls, handing one to Tryggve. I could see that it was weighty by the way it thumped when he dropped it to the ground. He unrolled the cloth to show us eight expertly crafted and sharpened blades and two scissors. "I made them from iron scraps I collected from the iron casters. The men said they did the same when they were young." He turned one over and I held out my hand to see it better. It even had some runic symbols carved in the handle.

Then it was Olav's turn to show what he brought. He had fashioned fishing nets from twine. The knots and edges were done in a way I had never seen before. "And I thought I was doing good to bring a piece of twine along." Edda laughed.

"Maybe we should just trade among ourselves," I replied. "You all brought such clever things."

"If we have items left over at the end of our stay, we can barter with each other," Tryggve suggested. "Kristin showed us the weavings you maids brought and they are fine as well."

"Edda," Kristin studied our friend. "Did you get those earrings today?"

"No, not today," she replied, looking steadily at Kristin.

"I do not remember seeing them before," Kristin replied.

Edda shrugged, "You are not very observant sometimes."

I looked from Kristin to Edda and sighed. Modir always says, "Let her tell her own story." I understood her to mean "Don't gossip." Oh, what a hard truth to obey. I bit my tongue, hoping that Edda would confide in Kristin at some point. The lads were busy admiring each other's craftsmanship.

"Do you think the mutton is done?" I asked. "I'm starving."

CHAPTER 12

We decided to roast all of the meat at once and overcook and salt what was left after we ate our fill so that it would keep. Hearing the music and singing from the colorful tents, the lads were eager to join the fun.

"Do you mind if we lads go this time?" asked Tryggve.

"I am tired anyway," I said. "Raven and I will stay here."

Edda quickly said, "I'll stay, too."

Kristin looked a bit disappointed, but probably didn't want to be the only maid going, so she said, "We will stay and clean up. Tomorrow I want to see everything."

After wrapping the meat and shaking out our blankets, I was weary from the long day and I lay by the embering fire resting my eyes while Kristin read aloud from the Bible. I heard Edda wander off toward the latrine. I dozed off and dreamed I heard a commotion and odd moaning sounds. Suddenly awake, I looked over and saw that Kristin was sleeping, Bible splayed on her chest. I lay still with my eyes wide open, waiting to hear the sounds again. Was someone in trouble? Raven was looking in the direction of the latrine with ears back and fur on end.

I sat up. Raven growled as footsteps approached. It was Edda. And I saw the back of a white-haired birch tree sneaking away.

"Edda…." I whispered. I did not know what I could say to her.

"I am tired. We should just go to sleep now," she said as she curled up on her blanket. Soon I heard her familiar snoring and I noted that I hadn't seen her limp even once since we arrived.

CHAPTER 13

Our days at Thingvellir were filled with so many sights and sounds. Musicians played, drums, flutes, horns, and stringed Langspil. Every day and night there was singing: some familiar songs I knew from Fadir or church or from the old women in the mountains, and some were new to me. I learned some sailing tunes and heard other songs in languages I didn't understand. The allure of Thingvellir brought people from everywhere to join in the trading and festivities.

There was lively dancing and -- after too much drinking -- there was fighting. Tryggve and Olav got drawn into such a fight with some other young men, but the next day, all was forgiven. I heard them entertaining each other by recounting the brawl of the night before, laughing all the while. "And then I put my fist to your nose. I did not know you could sneeze blood like that!"

I wished Ole could have seen the clowns, dressed in bright colors, making silly faces and doing funny things like pretending to remove my nose. One of the clowns was selling spinning tops and cups with handles that caught small wooden balls tethered to a string. I got one of each to bring home for Ole, and thought of the fun we would have playing together. I gawked at stilt-walkers, little dogs that jumped through hoops and danced, and wild animals: bears, wolves, badgers, all showing sharp teeth and claws behind the safety of the bars of strong cages. Kristin and Birgir visited the animals with me. Birgir brought out some small bits of cheese from his pocket and gamely held one at the wolves' cage. The two captive wolves lunged at the bars and Birgir dropped the cheese just in time to save his fingers from the snarling jaws. Kristin let out a sharp yell. A merchant strolling by shook his head and grinned, "That is the way to lose a hand, boy. Let that be a lesson to you."

I wanted to explore the market and festival areas by myself to see everything at my own pace. As long as I was careful and a bit wary, I knew I could fend for myself. Before coming to Thingvellir, I had heard stories of marauding men and pickpockets, but I did not experience any trouble. Throughout the week, I visited all of the market booths, even some with goods from foreign traders, like exotic dried spices and nuts. The merchants had brown faces and hands and bright white teeth. I imagined their homes as places of constant warmth and sunshine. Their hands were always beckoning. Smiling, they would call, "Come! Come! I give you a taste." The aromas were tantalizing. And the tastes were amazing. So different from the plain porridge, meat, and vegetables we ate at home. I traded two of my best woven belts for some spices for Modir and nuts for Fadir. I couldn't wait to see their faces when they tasted them.

I traded my sheep for an indulgence for myself: a wool cape with a white arctic fox collar. When I swung it around and fastened the clasp, I felt like a queen. When Edda saw it, she said the white fur was a fitting contrast to my dark hair, then she went and retrieved her sheep to trade for a similar cape for herself.

But the most memorable part of my time there was spent observing the law proceedings. I went with Tryggve, the only other one of our group who cared about Icelandic law. The rest of the group spent more of their time socializing. I figured I could socialize anytime, but this may be my only time to learn about law. I marveled at the memory of the Law Speaker who recited all of the laws of Iceland from the high Law Rock. The one who would take over from him was also there, learning as he listened. Next year, he would take his three-year turn as Law Speaker. Then he would be the one to call out the Chieftain's punishments for various crimes, including adultery, theft, and murder. Regardless of motive, the convicted killer was banished for three years from his or her home. If found by the victim's family, the family members were within their legal rights to kill the one who murdered their relative. Tryggve leaned over and whispered to me, "That's what happened to Erik the Red. He killed a man in a fit of temper and had to leave Norway for Iceland, then killed somebody in Iceland, too. He became quite the sea voyager, but more to stay alive than for the adventure."

The Law Speaker finished and we joined the other spectators as they moved outside the terraced area of the Logretta. Once all the chieftains and their cohorts were seated, the opening statement was issued with a thundering voice: "God will exact retribution from our whole society if sin and evil are allowed to flourish."

First, a cattle thief was sentenced to be hanged at Gallows Rock. His wife sobbed into her apron. "He only wanted to give our child some meat." I didn't go to witness the hanging, but Tryggve later told me that when the man dropped, he could hear the bones of his neck crack. Tryggve also told me that he witnessed a man who was beheaded with a blunt ax. The man had committed adultery and fathered a child in the illicit relationship.

The woman he sinned with was also sentenced. The adulteress, bearing a child from the man who was not her husband, was Olof Jonsdottir. It was discovered that she tried to cover up the sin by smothering and killing the baby. She was sentenced to drown along with another woman, Ragnihildur Tomasdottir, who was convicted of incest.

Our last day at Thingvellir was the day of the drowning. The festival atmosphere continued for all but those of us gathered at Drowning Pool at the base of a powerful waterfall. A long, thick rope stretched across the pool, drops of water reflecting the sunlight as they fell. Strong men gathered at each side of the pool, holding the ends of the rope. A strained hush fell over the crowd when muffled screams grew louder as three men carried a wool sack down to the water's edge. The woman inside continued to scream and struggle as they tied the sack to the rope spanning the water. Slowly, the men on one side gathered more rope as the men on the other side gave way. Once the sack was centered over the falls, they let the rope drop and I watched as the sack fell into the swirling eddy. Now the roar of the pelting falls overtook the sound of the screams. The sack went still, then sank. Soft sobs and groans from the witnesses also gathered in my throat.

The rope was retrieved and men were now coming with another sack. This woman was still and I wondered if she was already dead, but as they drew closer I heard her chanting in a low hoarse voice, "God, save me. Jesus, save me. Fadir, save me." Again, the men tied the sack to the rope and suddenly, the sack came alive, thrashing and screaming. But to no avail, of course. It dropped into the falls just like the one before it, and all sound stopped except for the sound of rushing water and muted sighs from the crowd.

Two women died in the Drowning Pool in 1705, and I witnessed them both. I will never forget the screams.

CHAPTER 14

That evening, while the others reveled on our last night away, I worried over all that I had witnessed, and when I tried to fall asleep, the darkness felt foreboding. A fitful sleep followed with troubling dreams of shadowy danger and morning seemed to come too soon. But the day had come for us to return to our homes. Kristin left our tent to help pack up the campsite and Edda and I were left alone to gather the tent's contents. Edda began in a low voice, "I traded the earrings for my fortune."

"You traded for coins?" I asked.

"Not coins. I visited a fortune-teller."

"How did you do that? Sooth-sayers are hanged."

"I was walking by a large rock where she was hidden. She put her hand out to me and whispered, "I have important message. You must hear."

"What did she say?"

"That I am with child."

"Edda! How can she know that?"

"I do not know. But I believe her. I am due for my bleeding and it has not come. I think I should tell Pjetur. He will want to marry me. He will have to."

I felt my heart pounding and my breakfast rising in my throat. "Maybe you should wait until you are sure?"

Edda continued folding clothes as if I had not spoken, "He will marry me and I will live in the fine yellow house with servants and beautiful things. His mother will admire my new cape. His father will be happy to have a baby in the house."

I held my tongue, but I was doubtful that the Arnesens would be openhearted to a kitchen servant as a dottir. Maybe the seer was wrong and just wanted to get Edda's earrings as payment for her lies. I thought of the drownings I witnessed and feared for Edda. Knowing my concerns would go unheeded, I replied with a vague, "Well, we will hope for the best."

We joined the others and saw that there was a sheep waiting by Raven. Instead of trading her sheep, Kristin traded weavings and her winning smile for some trinkets to bring home. "I want to be sure we have enough food for our journey back home," she said.

"You are the practical one," replied Edda.

Kristin smiled. "The Bible says we should think of others as more important than ourselves."

"Amen," said Birgir. "Besides, I like mutton for supper." He beamed at Kristin.

The six of us gathered our packs and, with the one sheep and Raven, set out with many other travelers heading north. I was not surprised when the twins did not join us that morning. Although we had seen them at evening parties at the Thing, they ignored us, spending their time with the chieftains, landowners, and the wealthy crowds. That was all fine with me. The less I saw of the twins, the better. I did see Edda sneak off that one night with Pjetur, though, and I wondered if she had seen him other times as well. Just the thought of it made my head hurt.

(HAPTER 15

Despite our tired walking, we made good progress on the first day. Groups of fellow travelers thinned as they broke off the trail to go in the direction of their homes. We decided to take a different route home than the one we took to arrive at Thingvellir so that we could see the legendary Gullfoss. When we reached the majestic golden falls, the sound of the falling water was deafening. "I want to stay here tonight," I shouted.

"Fine by me," replied Tryggve. "I could use a good night's rest after last night." He rubbed his forehead and frowned.

"We all could," replied Edda. "The last thing I need is another sore foot from too much walking."

"I am sorry you are not getting to ride home," Kristin sympathized.

"Uff da," I said under my breath.

"What did you say?" asked Edda.

"Nothing. I will hunt for game. Olav, might you have a net that you could use to get fish from the river?"

"I kept one. I did some special weaving on it, and had a hard time giving it up."

"I feel like that about some of my work, too," Tryggve said. "I kept a couple of my blades."

Birgir said, "I will help by telling stories while you two work." He laughed as the other boys gave him playful shoves. "Come on, then."

Kristin and Edda offered to stay and set up camp. I went to a nearby thicket and crouched in the underbrush to wait for prey. When I heard the muffled scream of a gull, I looked up. I loaded my slingshot and waited. Another scream, but it didn't sound like it was coming from above me. I stood and the hairs on my arms and neck did, too. That was a human scream. I ran to the campsite, fear making it difficult to breathe. As I got closer, I saw Edda curled on the ground, Pjetur kicking her head and belly with his hard boot. Edda wasn't the one screaming, it was Kristin. She stood a few feet away, her fists pounding her sides and screeching, "Stop it! Ogre! You will kill her!"

With my slingshot loaded and in my hand, my hunting reflex took over. I called, "Pjetur," and as he turned, the stone met its mark on his forehead. He dropped to the ground like felled timber. His head hit a rock and, with a surprised look in his open eyes, he was completely still. Blood seeped from his head onto the ground.

Kristin and I knelt by Edda. I brushed her hair from her face and gently shook her shoulder, "Edda! Edda!"

"Is she dead?" Kristin's voice shook.

I felt a catch in my throat. I could hardly breathe. Edda's right eye was swelling and a purple bruise was forming on a lump on her cheek. Tryggve, Olav, and Birgir came running then. "We thought we heard screams." Olav panted. Birgir went to Kristin who was trembling and put a comforting arm around her.

"What happened here?" Tryggve asked. He knelt by Pjetur and felt his neck. Tryggve's chin fell to his chest and then he slowly looked up. "Pjetur is dead."

CHAPTER 16

"What happened?" Olav and Tryggve asked at once. Words tumbled out as I recounted the screams, the kicking, the sling, the shot.

The lads began looking around in all directions. "Where is Einar?"

Kristin said, "When Pjetur rode up to us, he said Einar had gone on ahead. Pjetur wanted to know where all of you were, too. Edda grabbed his hand when he dismounted his horse and led him over by the falls. I couldn't hear what they were saying, but suddenly Pjetur hit Edda, knocking her to the ground and then he began to kick and kick her. It all happened so fast." Kristin was sobbing now.

Edda moaned and we ran to her side. "Wha.... Oh, my head …" She wiped some blood from her eye. "I am bleeding! What happened?"

As Edda slowly sat up, Kristin gently patted her back and said, "Lara saved you from Pjetur. He tried to kill you." Edda's face crumpled and she began to cry.

Tryggve took charge. "I think Edda will be all right. We can get her home on Pjetur's horse. But now we need to hide Pjetur's body and get Lara away in case Einar comes. Another traveler may have witnessed the killing. Lara's in danger."

Wide-eyed, I thought in alarm that only a few moments ago I was peacefully watching a beautiful waterfall. Now I was a fugitive. It was small comfort to know that I was right to be worried about Edda. Now I also needed to worry about myself.

Kristin grabbed my pack, pushed aside the waterproof cape and my new warm one to make room to stuff in her Bible. Tryggve slid in a long blade. Olav wound up the fishing net and put it in. Edda said, "Give her the twine from my pack and the extra dried fish."

Then Tryggve took out Edda's apron map and pointed south. "Go to the shore that way," he said, "It's the shortest route to the sea. You can't go east or you'll have to cross the Vatnajökull Glacier. That will kill you if Einar doesn't. "

"Be sure to hide along the way." Olav warned.

"Watch out for wild animals," Birgir said, no doubt thinking about his encounter with the caged wolves at the Thing. "And take the Vegvisir. Be safe." He patted my arm and handed me the carved stave along with his full water canteen.

In a flash of clear thought, I quickly I took from my pack the spices for Modir, the nuts for Fadir, and the toys for Ole. "Will you bring these to my family?"

Kristin reached for the packages, tears falling on them. "You are a hero."

"You can't return to home for at least three years," Olav reminded me. "Otherwise, the Arnesens will have your head."

In my dazed state, I tried to take it all in. "And take Raven," Tryggve added. "He will watch over you. Now go."

Birgir took Kristin's hand and she called, "We will pray for you every day!"

I couldn't believe what had happened; my life changed in an instant. What I thought was an adventure trip had become a sentence. I shouldered my full pack and resolutely walked away from my friends without looking back. Raven, seeming to understand his new job, came alongside me. Hot tears blurred my sight. I rubbed Raven's ears. His warm brown eyes met mine and he trotted ahead, leading the way.

CHAPTER 17

The sun had dimmed to its middle night's glow by the time I slowed my pace. When I stopped, I looked behind me and at every side and saw nothing but rocks, hills, and some brush. No people. It wasn't cold, but I shivered. What had I done and what would become of me? If not for the company of Raven, I would have been even more afraid, but I knew he would not only alert me to danger; he would try to protect me. I patted his warm black head and he looked back at me with an open smile. I felt the outline of my sling in my pocket and collected some rocks, to be ready in case of trouble or passing dinner. Fadir had tried to prepare me for trouble, but who could have anticipated this? When would I see Modir, Fadir, and little Ole again? What might the master do to them if he learned of Pjetur's death at my hand? I had to trust that my friends would not betray me. Surely Birgir, the storyteller, could concoct a plausible story to explain Pjetur's disappearance.

I walked more quickly again, hoping that Einar was not pursuing me on horseback. Approaching a large rock with a thicket of briars alongside, something colorful caught my eye. There, tucked near the base of the rock, was a basket roughly woven of leaves and sticks, and inside was an assortment of colorful wild berries. My mouth watered as I pushed Raven's snout away. Did this belong to someone?

Was it a trap? The sight of the berries made my empty stomach growl. I looked all around. I saw no one. I quickly snatched the basket and gobbled the berries. My aching hunger subsided and I washed the berries down with some sips of water from Birgir's canteen. I wanted to gulp more, but I didn't know when I would find fresh water again. Raven's sad eyes told me that he was hungry and thirsty, too. "You'll have to find your own food, Friend," I swept my hand toward the vast landscape. Raven took off running and I prayed to Jesus that he would return to me. As I saw his figure disappearing in the dusky light, I was immediately lonely and sorry I didn't have food and water to share so Raven could stay close. I had to conserve my meager supplies, not knowing how long it would take for me to reach Iceland's shore.

I decided to wait for Raven by the big rock and try to sleep some. It felt good to set down my pack that had grown heavier with my weariness. I laid out my cape and removed my boots. My stockings were damp, so I laid them out on the rock to dry while I rested -- cool air on my feet. Using some of the briars and striking together two sharp rocks, I built a small fire. Using my shawl for a blanket, and Kristin's Bible for a pillow, I held my blade in my palm and closed my eyes.

I must have fallen asleep immediately, because I was startled from a pleasant dream about talking animals when Raven returned, panting loudly. He dropped a water bird by my hand and ran away again. I sat up and looked at the limp bird. Quickly, I plucked its feathers, skewered it on a stick, and roasted it on the remaining embers of the fire. I couldn't wait for it to be fully cooked, and burned my mouth on the hot meat. I ate quickly and as I was wiping the grease from my chin, Raven returned with another bird for himself. He crouched down near the dying fire and tore into it with gusto. "Good boy." I praised my companion for providing for both of us. I drank a bit from the canteen and poured some in my cupped hand for Raven. He lapped it up in a second and looked expectantly at me. "If you found water birds, there must be water nearby. Can you wait until I've rested a bit more? Then we can look for it together." Obediently, Raven lowered his head onto his front paws and looked at me from under his brows. "Good night, sweet Raven. Sleep well." As I drifted off to sleep, Raven snuggled in by my feet.

CHAPTER 18

When I awoke to slant light, I saw a bulging animal skin at my side. I sat up quickly and moved away from it. On looking more closely, I saw that it was a skin filled with something. I heard a noise and looked up. In a thicket a stone's throw away, my eye caught a flicker of something brown retreating. I squinted and made out the shape of – maybe a very large rabbit? It was ambling away on outstretched back legs. "Oh," I murmured and the creature dropped to all fours and turned toward me. Large dark eyes peered back and whiskered cheeks, chin, and brows quivered. As my eyes adjusted, I could see the creature a bit more clearly. It was wearing a brown vest and pointed hat. Could the hat be concealing tall ears? As I watched, the creature reached up and lightly tugged the brim of the hat, then turned and disappeared in the thicket. My heart was still beating hard. I wondered how the creature had been so stealthy not to awaken Raven who snored peacefully at my feet.

I once again turned my attention to the curious animal skin. It was a supple tanned hide cinched with a leather strap. What might be inside? I tentatively poked it. Slosh. Curiosity overcame my fear and I began to untie the bag. Now Raven was awake and sniffed and pawed as I worked the tie loose. As soon as an opening appeared, Raven began to lap its contents. I put my finger in and tasted. Fresh water – not at all brackish, but cool and refreshing.

Could this creature also have left me the berries? Modir told stories of Huldufólk, the hidden folk who lived in and under large rocks. We always took care not to disturb their rocky homes. Fadir said no one could see them with their eyes, only in visions and dreams. I pinched the back of my hand to be sure I was awake and flinched. Raven jumped and hunkered down, ready to pounce.

"Good dog, Raven." I stroked his head and scratched his chin. Now that we were both wide awake, I put on my dry socks and boots and rearranged my pack so I could also carry the water skin, all the while wondering at the kindness of the mysterious creature.

CHAPTER 19

Raven and I set off in the direction where I last saw the creature, sensing that it was the way to the sea. I kept a lookout for the creature, but perhaps it was hiding or much faster than we were. It was difficult to judge our direction since the sun never really set, but soon a glow appeared in the east and I was assured that our path continued south to the sea.

After a time, we stopped and drank the water we were given and also ate the dried fish in my pack. I hoped to catch some fresh fish or water birds as we got closer to the sea. Soon we saw a rivulet and followed it. Then, in the far distance, I saw a great expanse of white. The sight of the icy glacier confirmed what Tryggve had told me about our route. Underfoot, the terrain began to be more like dark gravel: the moraine area of the huge glacier. I veered right and continued my path south, the rivulet becoming a stream. Raven eagerly lapped from the cold stream and I knelt, cupped my hands and did the same before refilling Birgir's canteen and the animal skin.

When I rose from the stream's banks, I glimpsed brown fur emerging from behind a nearby thicket. My creature friend. This time, our eyes met directly and the creature lifted an arm to beckon me. Cautiously, I began to walk toward it. Raven walked by my side, his demeanor one of deference and respect. As I drew closer, I saw that the creature had breasts under the vest and a flower adorning the tall hat. A female creature! Now I felt less apprehensive and walked a bit faster, but as we got closer, she turned and loped away. Then she stopped, looked back to see that we followed her, and beckoned us on. We never lost sight of her and in what seemed like a short time, we saw the seashore in the distance. Raven galloped on ahead. The creature saw him coming and kept pace ahead of him until they reached the rocky shore.

When I joined them, I was out of breath, but could not help but laugh. What a comical pair they made. Raven nuzzled the creature and she patted his head, just barely shorter than her shoulder. What happened next surprised me: the creature spoke.

CHAPTER 20

"Hei Hei," she said.

I nearly fell over and choked on my laughter. Her voice was rough, but soft. I had to strain to hear her words. Strangely, I sensed them more inside my head than in my ears. I tentatively replied, "Hei."

The creature continued, her soft brown eyes looking intently into mine beneath her long eyelashes. "I was at Gullfoss. I saw. I help you." She paused, her whiskered nose quivered. "You are Lara."

"I am."

"I am Hildur. Come." I followed her to some rocks and tall grass at the water's edge. There she pointed to a raft. "Take it."

Raven immediately ran to the raft and jumped on it. He turned and looked at me with his tongue hanging out and eyes shining. "Right now?" I hesitated.

"Now. Einar comes." She motioned with her arms and took a few steps back. I turned and looked out at the great gray expanse of water and felt my belly tighten. Fadir had taken me sailing and taught me to fish, but always in the shelter of the fjord and near shallow areas. This sea looked like a never-ending swell that could easily swallow a raft made of driftwood. But, if I stayed, I would face Einar's cruel punishment or imprisonment until next year's Althing when I would likely be drowned.

So, my choices were certain death or probable death. I climbed onto the raft.

CHAPTER 21

Hildur gave the raft a heave and we were afloat. Immediately we began to drift away from the shore. I knew that if I didn't try to quickly wrest control of the raft, we would hit rocks near the shore. With shaking hands, I fetched Birgir's Vegvisir from my pack to use as a rudder. The raft had a mast, so I got out Modir's waterproof cape and Edda's twine and affixed the cape as a sail to the mast. When I looked back at the shore, Hildur was gone. I waved goodbye anyway. It seemed like the least I could do.

Raven settled himself near the center of the raft and I did the same. We bobbed along among the waves and I adjusted our angle to head east, knowing that Norway was in that direction. My best hope was to make it back to my Fadir and Modir's homeland and find family there to help me. The sail and the wind cooperated. I looked back at Iceland's shore and saw the great expanse of the Vatnajökull Glacier rising from the sea up to the mountains. After some time, the glacier was behind me. The land flattened and receded. The sun didn't set, but dimmed and the white-capped waves grew. The raft rocked and pitched the farther we got out into the sea. Iceland got smaller and smaller until it disappeared. Birds circled around us and dove like arrows into the sea, spearing fish with their long beaks. In my pack, I found one last piece of dried fish, set a bit of it on the raft, and held Olav's net, willing a bird to alight so I could snare it. Raven crept nearer and nearer the fish and sniffed it. "No Raven!" I admonished. I couldn't let him eat our bait. He ventured his tongue out for a taste. I spanked his nose. He looked at me as if I were the worst traitor anywhere. "Awww." I scratched under his chin. "I know. I'm hungry, too. I'll share the bird when I catch it," I assured him. He settled down with his head on his paws, his watchful eyes darting about. He was willing a bird to land, too.

A gust of wind blew the bit of fish off the raft and we both looked mournfully over the side of the raft. The bait was slowly sinking when a flash of silver approached the bait, swam away and returned. I quickly readied the net and snagged a beautiful cod, then hauled the heavy fish onto the raft. My strength was nearly spent after I used Vegvisir to club the fish so it would not fling itself back into the sea. I sat back, breathing hard, and grinned. "What do you think of that?" I asked Raven. He stood on the raft, legs splayed to stay steady and let the drool fall from his tongue onto the fish. I carefully removed the net and set about cleaning the fish with my small blade. Then I remembered the larger blade that Tryggve had given me and I made quick work of the job. Raven and I had our fill and I washed the remains into the sea. We drank sparingly from our water supply, saving as much as I could. With a full belly, exhaustion washed over me. The waves settled some, so I got out my cape and drew Raven close. I folded the sail to slow the raft. We snuggled in the middle, covered up, and I hoped to sleep. Lying under the cape with Raven, I looked out over the sea. The night was clear, the moon and stars shown brightly in the dim light. Waves sparkled. If we were not in danger, it would have been a most lovely ride. The waves slowly rocked us and the last thing I remembered was Raven's gentle snoring.

CHAPTER 22

I dreamed of the small whiskered woman. She was with Modir, Fadir, and Ole. They were all holding hands and singing a quiet tune together. It was a tune I didn't know, but they all seemed familiar with it – even young Ole. I couldn't make out the words except at the end. It sounded like "Amen."

"Ahoy!" I woke with a start. My eyes flew open and then I remembered that I was floating on the sea. Raven scrambled to his feet and began barking in earnest. I sat up and shielded my eyes to see the shadow of something alongside the raft. A fishing boat! "Gather your things and come aboard. Hildur sent us."

Still groggy from sleep, I shook my head and looked at the maid who was speaking to me. "Wha... who are you?"

"I am Runa and this is my brodur Runi." She leaned over the edge of the boat and extended her arm to me. "Give me your hand. Or your pack. Or your dog. Let me help you." Raven did not need another invitation. He threw himself into her arms with such gusto that she fell back into the boat, laughing.

I felt like I was still in a dream. "Hildur sent you?"

"Ja. Now, come along. We are working folks and don't have time for all this talking."

Dutifully, I handed her my pack, grabbed the cape from the mast and Runi reached down and easily lifted me from the raft onto the boat. Strong and efficient, Runa lassoed a rope onto the raft and Runi hoisted their sail. Off we sped, with the raft in tow. My head was spinning. I tried to make sense of my new circumstances. When was it that I was with my friends returning from Thingvellir? How long had I been floating? The world tilted and shifted. My vision dimmed and then all went black.

CHAPTER 23
KIRKJUBOUR FAROE ISLANDS

I awoke in a bed inside a cozy wooden cabinet with a sliding door: a badsofa. When I slid the door open, Raven nuzzled my face. What a comfort to wake to my faithful companion. I sat up and looked around the unfamiliar house. "Hei Hei," I called, tentatively. Where was I and how did I get here?

Slowly, the memory of my flight from Iceland re-formed in my mind, and finally I remembered being rescued from the sea in the fishing boat. I startled as the door of the hut opened and an old woman, bent and shuffling, entered with a basket of laundry. She peered at me in the dark house, her eyes adjusting from the bright outdoors. "Ah, and there she is," she smiled. "Welcome to our home."

"Thank you." I rubbed the sleep from my eyes. "Are you family to Runa and Runi?"

"Ja. My dottir and sonur."

"How long have I been here? Where am I?"

"Questions and answers. They brought you in two days ago. You must have been powerfully tired to sleep so soundly for so long. You are at Kirkjubour on the Faroe Islands. I fed your dog. Does he have a name?" At this, Raven went to the woman for an expected scratch under his chin.

"He is Raven. And I am Lara."

"Ja. Hildur told me your name. Call me Agnas."

"Hildur…. But she is in Iceland."

"She comes to me in my dreams. She is a friend. And now you must have food and drink. Here is some skyr with berries." I looked hungrily at the waiting bowl and stood, but my feet buckled and I fell back onto the bed. "You are parched and hungry and need to regain your land legs. Go slow."

I marveled at the kindness of my rescuers. The Faroe Islands. I had heard about the islands when I was a child. A visiting sailor from the Faroes told stories around a campfire one summer night. Modir said their stories reminded her of the Norwegian tales of elves and trolls.

I rose slowly and took two steps to the table. Remembering my manners, I folded my hands and bowed my head, reciting the prayer I learned at home: "For all thy blessings, known and unknown, remembered and forgotten, I give You thanks. Amen." I looked up at Agnas. "And thank you."

She waved my words aside. "We are really just old Norse folk and we adhere to Norsemen sayings. Do you know this one? 'A guest needs the giving of water, fine towels, and friendliness.' "

I smiled at the familiar saying. "Ja. My modir also says it. She says hospitality is one of the ancient virtues." I held my spoon above the bowl, waiting for our conversation to end.

"And patience is another ancient virtue, but you arc hungry. Eat!" Agnas said, "We will have plenty of time for talk after."

Gratefully, I gobbled the food, looking around the hut as I ate. It was small, about the size of my Iceland home, but there was no loft. It was constructed of stone with a sod roof. Badsofas lined both sides of the outer walls. The table with small benches where I now ate was in the center.

At the end of the room were the hearth, cooking pot, and two rocking chairs, made of unfinished gray wood. With Raven at her feet, Agnas sat in one of the chairs and, as I finished the last of the cup of fresh water, she motioned for me to join her.

"Now, Child," she began, "Hildur hinted that there was trouble for you back in Iceland. You are not required to tell anyone here anything about it. You are safe here and you may stay as long as you want to." Agnas smiled, leaned forward, and gently squeezed my hand. "We will put you to work, of course."

"Of course," I replied. I did not expect to be waited on.

"Runa and Runi are away most days with the fishing. That is our livelihood. But we also have a garden and sheep and a house to keep." Agnas chuckled, "And I am not getting any younger." She smoothed her unruly gray hair from her brow and tucked it under her brown kerchief.

"I am used to hard work," I said.

Agnas lightly clapped together her wrinkled and gnarled hands. "Wonderful girl," she said. "Today is beautiful and sunny. Come outside so I can show you around and then we will find some tasks to fill your day."

Feeling strong and steady now, I stood. Agnas took my hand and Raven jumped up in expectation. Agnas opened the door and sunshine fell on us.

CHAPTER 24

With his tail high and waving in the breeze, Raven followed us outside. I squinted as my eyes adjusted to the bright sunshine and saw that we were at the top of a hill leading higher to a mountain. Below us was an expanse of sea with a harbor, and near the shore a church, longhouse, and graveyard. Agnas swept her arm at the view. "Welcome to Kirkjubour." Her eyes shone.

I heard the sound of the bellwether before I saw the sheep. Raven immediately saw his job and circled around the last of the sheep, encouraging them to keep up. "Wonderful dog," Agnas said. "We have not had a sheepdog in many years." The bellwether ram pushed his head under Agnas' hand and she held his horn. "This is St. Luke. Some think it's sacrilege to name a sheep for a saint, but he has earned the title." She scratched the ram's neck and crooned, "Good boy. Come. I will show you the garden." Behind the hut was a terraced area leading up the mountainside. "Potatoes." She said. "We must maintain the fence. The sheep are drawn to the greens." Agnas shook her head and clucked in dismay. "But this autumn, if you can stay, you can help us dig."

"We have Potato Week in Iceland, too," I said. "Everyone helps, and we shear and slaughter sheep then, too."

"Ja. Cold winters require provisions. I often wonder about folks who live in places that are warm all year. I have heard tales of such places from traders with brown skin and bright smiles." She chuckled. "Maybe we would smile more if we were warm all year, too. Here. You can take the rest of the dry laundry off the clothesline and carry the basket in the house. It is becoming more and more difficult for me to walk and carry a load. Bad knees," she explained.

Trousers, shifts, bedclothes, and towels waved in the breeze. Most were shades of brown, so it was hard to know by looking at them that they were really clean, but the sun and breeze gave them a fresh aroma. St. Luke nudged my leg and then worked his head under my hand. I took hold of his horn and moved his smelly head away from the clean laundry. The warmth of the horn near his head brought my thoughts back home. I wondered if my friends had arrived back to the farms. I wondered how Modir, Fadir, and Ole fared.

"Look there!" Agnas interrupted my thoughts, "Runa and Runi in their boat, coming back. Bring the basket to the hut and we will go down to see their catch." I saw a boat approaching the mouth of the fjord and marveled that Agnas could know it was her people from so far away. I hurried the basket into the hut and joined Agnas who was already heading down the hillside. Agnas struggled to make her way down the rocky slope, so I offered my arm. "Bless you, dear," she said.

⟨HAPTER 25⟩

When Agnas and I reached the boat, there were already some folks from the village gathered to barter for fresh fish for their dinner. Runi hauled three baskets of fish onto shore while Runa carefully folded the nets and gathered their gear. A mother with a baby balanced on her hip asked, "Will you take this fresh loaf of bread for that large cod?" Runi nodded and made the exchange. Another man traded ptarmigan eggs, and a young girl traded spun wool for fish.

Raven ran in circles around the group and then nudged Runa when she climbed from the boat. Runa rubbed Raven's head. Then she turned to me, "Ja. I see you are back with the living. And now we take the rest of the fish to the drying shed." Runa, Runi, and I each shouldered a basket and we made our way back up the hill. St. Luke appeared and Agnas held his horn to steady her climb.

Alongside the hut was a wooden building with gaps between the upright siding boards. A rough table stood just outside the door. "Set the basket here." She pointed next to the table. "Watch and learn." Then she drew a knife from her belt and quickly beheaded and slit each fish, flipping the heads into a waiting basket and handing the fileted fish to Runi who deftly tied a reed onto the tail and hung it from a crossbeam in the shed. I was impressed by their efficiency, but also by the bounty of drying meat in the shed. I recognized parts of sheep, fish, and birds.

"Here," Runa thrust a fish into my hands. "Help Runi keep up." She continued to chop, chop, chop in a steady rhythm and Runi strung up three fish to my one. "You will get faster," Runa glanced at my fumbling fingers.

Agnas caught fish heads that flew beyond the basket before Raven could snatch them. "These I will boil for stew," she explained a bit out of breath.

"I have seen the open-air fish drying racks back at home in Iceland, but I never saw the work to hang them. We are farmers," I explained. "We barter for dried fish."

Agnas said, "Ja. Farmers are important, too."

A reed broke when I tried to tie it too tightly. Runi took my hands and patiently guided them to make a good knot. I grabbed another fish and tried again. This process reminded me of learning to weave as a young girl. I did some sloppy work before I learned to do it well. When the last fish was hung, Runi picked up the fish head basket and threw two large heads on the ground on his way into the hut. Raven knew they were for him; he delicately dissected the fish with his teeth, gobbling the flesh and leaving the bones. Runa showed me their small outhouse and washing pool fed by a nearby cascade from the mountain. "You have time before our meal if you would like to wash up. I will bring you a clean shift."

"Takk. But I have extra clothes in my pack that I washed at Althing. I will fetch my pack."

I started for the hut but Runa called, "Wait. You were at Althing?"

"Ja. With friends. It was our turn to go this year."

"But Althing is not happening until the next moon phase." Runa said.

I thought about what she said and realized we were talking about two different events. "The Faroese have Althing, too? I was at Iceland's Althing."

I could see that Runa was turning this revelation over in her mind. "Ah, of course. We plan to go to the Faroe Althing in Torshavn soon. Perhaps you can go with us."

"Hmmmm," I said without enthusiasm. The drownings and Pjetur's death tainted my enthusiasm for the Althing. "I will just go get my pack now." I headed back to the hut.

CHAPTER 26

Raven paced in and out of the door that Agnas had propped open. The fish heads boiling in the large kettle over the hearth created heat and steam.

"I came to get my pack," I said as I entered.

"You are not leaving us, I hope," said Agnas.

"Nei. Just fetching clean clothes."

"Good. We will eat soon," Agnas smiled and stirred the pot.

After bathing, I combed and plaited my hair and returned to the hut, feeling refreshed. Runi and Runa were already sitting at the table and Agnas was ladling hot soup into bowls. "Come and sit," Runa said.

We gave thanks for our meal and began to slurp the fish broth. Runi looked steadily at me as he passed the fresh loaf of bread. I broke off a piece and dipped it into my soup bowl. How good it felt to eat with a family once again. My eyes filled and salty tears fell into my soup. I swallowed a spoonful of the broth in spite of the lump in my throat. Agnas reached over and squeezed my hand. Her hands were gnarled but strong and seemed a little large for her small, wiry frame. Unruly gray hair tucked under a brown headscarf framed her pale cheeks. She winked at me and continued to eat. Runi had bright blue eyes and thick yellow hair that reminded me of tufts of wild grass. His broad shoulders and large rough hands were those of a hard worker. He had a big appetite and helped himself to more soup before I had eaten even half of my portion. He glanced at me while I was appraising him and I caught a small smile. Runa was unlike any woman I had known. She was nearly as tall as Runi and just as strong. The small braids gathered from the front to the back of her head barely held her haystack of long yellow tresses. She had offered a maid's shift to me, but she was dressed like a man in trousers and a short tunic gathered by a wide leather belt that held her knife and keys. She was not unkind, but she was not warm and friendly like her modir. Her gray eyes met mine as I studied her. "Tell us about your home. And what are your skills?" she asked.

I swallowed and told of Fadir, Modir, and Ole at home. "I help take care of Ole," I explained, "I keep house, and help with the garden and the animals."

"And your skills? Do you fish?"

"Fadir has taken me to fish in the fjord, but not often. I spin and weave." I hesitated. "And I can hunt. With a sling."

Their heads all snapped up to look at me then. Runa spoke, "That is an unusual skill for a maid."

"Ja," I changed the subject. "The soup is delicious, Agnas. Thank you for food."

Raven barked insistently just outside the hut. Runi rose to look. "It is Fadir approaching," he said.

Agnas rose to fill another bowl. "Well!" She said. "This is a surprise."

CHAPTER 27

With crunch of gravel and a shadow at the door, the newcomer arrived. Not hearing any mention of him before now, I had assumed that the fadir had died, but here he was, his large figure filling the hut's doorway. Runi went to the door. The fadir's booming voice rose over Raven's barking, "What, dottir? You do not stand to greet your fadir?"

Runa slowly stood and fixed a hard stare at the man. "That is better. Woman, do you have food for me?" Runa sat again and slurped her soup.

Agnas hustled a bowl of soup and what was left of the bread to the place where she had been sitting and quickly cleared her own bowl away. The big man sat at the table, took a bite of the bread, and addressed me with a full mouth. "And who is this sitting at my table?"

Agnas answered before I could open my mouth. "She is Lara, a visitor sent by Hildur."

"By Hildur, you say? We best be cordial then, I reckon." He looked my way with a forced smile. "The huldufolk are looking out for you. Interesting." He did not really seem interested. Runa kept her head bent over her bowl. Runi crouched down to calm Raven. The fadir continued, "So! I supposed you are wondering why I am here." He looked at each face and then shrugged, "I will tell you. I am leaving for a long trading voyage once the Thing is over, so I am getting provisions. Then I will leave you to your little lives again." He laughed as if he had told a dirty joke. No one else laughed. Only Agnas looked at him. I wondered why a sweet, kind woman ever married such a man. Perhaps he had not always carried so much weight around his belly. Perhaps his leathery face, now covered with a grizzled untrimmed beard had once been handsome. Perhaps he had once been good-humored and charming. But the way he was now only furthered my resolve not to make a poor marriage choice. How does one know who is a good choice? My own modir and fadir were both fine, principled folk who care for each other. Was that an exception in marriage? I studied Agnas' face. What I saw there was a mixture of fear and worry. I would not be the only one glad to see him leave the hut once more.

"Tell me what you need," said Agnas. "I will get it for you."

"I will get it myself. Bring me a sturdy sack, Woman," he replied.

He swung the empty sack over his shoulder on his way to the drying shed. "He had better not take all of our meat," Runa said quietly.

"Hush," Agnas whispered. "We have always made up for his excesses. We will manage this time, too." Runi quietly led Raven inside the hut and closed the door.

And then, to my surprise, quiet, taciturn Runi spoke.

CHAPTER 28

"He will take what he wants whether we allow him or not. Just let him get what he wants and go," Runi spoke quietly but urgently, a look of concern on his brow. "Please, Runa, just keep still. He will only make trouble for you if you object."

"My jaw aches with all I want to say to him," Runa hissed. "But if keeping quiet will appease the ogre, I will do it for your sakes, not his." She stood and snatched her bowl from the table. "I will wash up. Keeping busy will help my mind not to wander into troublesome territory."

I wondered what their fadir had done to them in the past. I doubted that pilfering their hard-earned provisions was their only reason to fear him. They were more than generous to me, a stranger. I was curious, but did not think I should pry, especially with the fadir still so close that he might overhear. I picked up my bowl and went to help Runa with the washing up. Agnas absently stirred the pot, then went to the window, and back to the hearth where she sat and picked up her knitting with shaking hands. "He is at the root cellar now," she whispered. "I hope he can find enough among last year's crop to satisfy him." She looped the yarn over the knitting needle but had trouble making the stitch. She tried again, and then put the knitting back, in the basket and kneaded her hands in her lap. Her face held a pained expression. Raven's toenails click-clicked on the floor as he made his way over to her and nudged her hands with his nose. Agnas petted Raven's black head until he smiled with pleasure.

The door to the hut slammed open. We all jumped. Raven barked. The fadir dropped his food sack to the floor and slammed the door shut again. "Shut that dog up. Fetch my extra clothes." he shouted. As he neared, I could smell his foul breath. He threw a grimy, bulging sack at Agnas. "See that these are clean and mended when I return."

Agnas left the sack where it landed and piled his clean clothes onto a blanket. "Do you want all of them?"

"What do you think? That I am going to wash my clothes myself? Give me all of them."

Her shaky hands passed the bundle to him. "When will you return?" Agnas asked softly.

"When I am good and ready and not before. Just get it done before I come back."

Runi went to the door and opened it. "You are ready to go now."

The fadir looked at Runi with slitted eyes and lowered brows. Fully regarding Runi's stature and bearing, he straightened his back to full height and puffed out his chest, but he did not measure up to Runi. The two men stared at each other. Runi did not blink. Finally the old man picked up his provisions and slammed his shoulder into Runi's on his way out. Runi quietly closed the door, then took one of the chairs and wedged it under the latch. We all crowded around the window and watched the fadir lumber down the hill and out of sight. Runa let out a long sigh. Agnas patted Runi's back, then rubbed Runa's arm. I sat down hard on a bench and blinked slowly, willing my heart to beat a more regular rhythm. Dealing with a man like that might be the kind of thing that would make a person drink spirits. I wished I could ask my own dear fadir about that.

CHAPTER 29

Everyone was pensive and quiet after the fadir's visit and the rest of the afternoon and evening found us puttering around in the hut. Runi repaired an old fishing net and whittled what might be the figure of an animal. Runa scraped some hides that had been soaking in the urine barrel. I cleaned and teased wool to prepare it for spinning. I had a basket by my side with the cleaned wool and a rag in my lap to catch the bugs, clumps of dirt, straw, and burrs I removed from the raw wool. This was a mindless task during which my modir at home would tell stories or we would sing. Today I was quiet and listened to Agnas hum tunelessly while she ground wheat in a stone bowl and then rolled and kneaded dough for bread. While she waited for the dough to rise, she joined me by the hearth and picked up her knitting, which she now deftly worked with calm fingers. Soon Runa and Runi pulled up a bench and joined us. We worked in silence for some time, Raven going from one person to another, curious to know what we were doing and no doubt hoping it involved a treat or petting for him.

Finally, Agnas broke the silence. "Lara, I suppose you are wondering about my husband." I started to deny my curiosity, but she interrupted me. "No, I know he's a scoundrel, but he was not always that way."

"Ja, he was," Runa said.

Agnas ignored Runa's objection, "When I first met Johan, he was full of fun, always joking and laughing. And he was handsome. All the girls thought so. Just look at Runi. That's what Johan looked like." Runi made a face and color rose in his cheeks. Agnas said, "But, of course, Runi is even more handsome." Runa chuckled. Agnas continued, "When I first saw Johan, it was at a special church gathering in Torshavn. The preacher had just welcomed everyone when the door opened and in walked this tall sailor. He had a broad smile and walked down the aisle with confidence to the very front pew. I could not keep from looking at his wavy hair and broad shoulders all through the church service. After the last "Amen," there was a picnic and I joined my friends, whispering and giggling about the stranger. Suddenly, all the girls stopped talking and with wide eyes looked above my head. I turned to see him behind me. 'What is so funny?' he asked. All the girls ran away. Except me. We walked around the picnic grounds together and talked. He told me that he was a sailor with a shipping company that traded all over the world. He had grand ideas about visiting exotic places, but mostly his work had just taken him to Denmark and Norway. I was enthralled to meet a man who had been anywhere but the Faroe Islands and he entertained me with tales of kings and queens, cities and castles, sweets and finery. The next day he set sail again, but not before asking where I lived. And I lived right here, in this very hut, with my modir, fadir, and sister."

"But her sister died," Runa said.

"Ja. It was very sad. The winter after I met Johan, my sister died of a breathing sickness. I remember waking up to hear her coughing until she spit blood. She was buried in the spring." Agnas paused and wiped her eye with the back of her hand. "I loved her. She was my first and best friend."

"I am sorry to hear that she died," I said. "What about your modir and fadir?"

"Well, they both lived to be a little older than I am now. First Fadir passed, and then Modir. From hard work and old age. Their graves are by my sister's in the churchyard by the shore." Agnas nodded and rocked in her chair as she knitted.

Runi spoke then. "Fadir was always mean, from what I remember."

"Ja, and I am sad about that," Agnas said. "He never adjusted to having a wife and children. He has a wandering spirit."

"A wandering spirit? That is what you call it?" said Runa, "I call it a short temper and a ready fist."

"You are right, Dottir," Agnas said. "I can not defend him. He was not a good fadir to you."

"He is still not a good fadir," Runa said.

Agnas agreed, "Ja, but we can take comfort in the long times he is away."

Runi spoke up, "I would that he never came back."

Agnas put her knitting in her lap and leaned forward. "I do not like to wish someone ill, but Hildur came to me in a dream. She showed me a grave with his name on it."

"From your mouth to God's ears," said Runa.

"Amen," said Runi.

Agnas stood and brushed the wrinkles from her apron, "And now I bake the bread."

CHAPTER 30

The next morning arrived in what felt like the middle of the night. Runa opened the door to my badsofa and shook my shoulder. "Come fish with us," she said. I rose up on my elbow and yawned. I rose slowly and put on my boots that were warm from Raven sleeping on them. I tried to keep pace with Runa and Runi while they gobbled their skyr. "We need to get on the water early," Runa explained. "The best fishing is at dawn."

I found it was hard to tell exactly when the sun rose during the summer midnight sun, but I was sure that if anyone knew when to fish, it was these two. Agnas cleared the table while we gathered gear, including a boiled potato for each of our pockets and a canteen of fresh water that Runi held out for me to carry. He did not immediately let go after I had taken hold. He blinked and turned. I followed him to the shore.

Once in the boat, Runi and Runa worked together in a way only those who have teamed up over many years can do. They extended the nets and handed hooks and ropes back and forth without a word. I sat in the middle, hanging onto a plank as the sails caught wind and the boat sped over waves. Runi adjusted the sails without missing a hand-off from Runa. I was astounded at their efficiency and skill and wondered what I could possibly do to be of any help. As if she read my mind, Runa called to me above the wind, "Once we begin to haul the nets in, you will help pull the fish in and secure them under the net in the bottom of the boat." I nodded and readied myself. Along the horizon, I saw a shelf of gray. Runi glanced my way, then raised his hand over his brow and saw it, too. He tugged Runa's sleeve and pointed. Runa frowned. Runi nodded almost imperceptibly to her, and they simultaneously dropped the net over the side of the boat. I felt the pull on that side and instinctively leaned the other way. Runi and Runa leaned back as well and then, with a mighty heave, pulled the net full of fish into the boat. They deftly flipped the net and I lay on top of it to capture the jumping fish. A few escaped over the side before I secured the rest. Runi said, "Good." He was a man of few words, but when he spoke, it meant something. "Now we try to beat the storm." With that, he adjusted the sails and he and Runa each grabbed an oar and began rowing back toward the safety of the fjord and bay. With each pummeling wave, the boat pitched and lunged. I felt helpless and imagined that Runa and Runi's muscles ached and burned with each stroke of the oars.

"Loosen the sail before it pulls us over!" Runa shouted. I crawled to the mast and held it with one hand while I stood on my toes to reach the top of the sail. I lost my balance and tried to grab the mast with my free hand, but missed and fell onto the fish. I scrambled up again and this time was able to loosen the sail. The net holding the fish rose and fell with the waves. I held the net as well as I could over the fish to keep them from falling out. Then I sat on top of it all while front of the boat rose high into the air and then smacked down over and over with the big waves. I had to turn my face away from the fierce wind to be able to see. Lightning flashed across the sky and crack of thunder resounded in my chest. Rain fell like a mighty waterfall. I crawled over to a bucket and began to bail water. I thought, I survived the wrath of Einar in Iceland, but now this is how I will die. Water began to slosh over each side of the boat, but the fish remained. I could not account for the strange phenomenon. I continued to bail, but the sloshing action took the rain out of the boat as quickly as it fell. I looked toward the bay and, with the next flash of lightning, saw the shore and on it, a small figure valiantly waving a piece of cloth. Runa and Runi were completely drenched. Through their wet sleeves, I could see their muscles straining with each pull of the oars. I felt like we had been caught in the storm for hours, making such small progress with each passing moment. But finally, I could see that the small waving figure was Agnas. We approached in slow but sure measure and I was shocked when Runa and Runi suddenly dropped the oars and jumped out. Were they abandoning me? I got up on my knees and saw that they were up to their shoulders in the water. Runi grabbed the rope at the front of the boat and Runa held the side as they slowly pulled and guided the boat to the shore. I was relieved when I saw their belts emerged from the water, then their legs, and finally Runi ran up onto the shore and the two of them pulled the boat far up to safety and secured it, with me just hanging on, sitting on top of the pile of fish. Runi tipped the boat on its side. "Get out," he called. He did not have to tell me twice. I fell onto my knees on the rocky shore and watched while they dumped the fish onto the sail cloth. They gathered up the sides and, with each of us taking a corner, we made our way up the hillside. Even after all the rowing, Agnas and I were no match for the strength of the other two, but after a few stumbles, we got the fish up to the drying hut and dropped the whole load inside before running to the shelter of the hut. We were all drenched and the potato in my pocket was smashed all to bits.

CHAPTER 31

After surviving the big storm, I asked to be given chores on land. I spent the following days dyeing and spinning wool, tending sheep with Raven, gardening, and helping Agnas with household tasks like cooking and cleaning. On Saturday night, we all bathed and put on clean clothes and on Sunday morning after breakfast, Agnes held a basket.

"Will you carry this? There is a picnic after church." As a family, we walked down the rocky hill to the church, dodging sheep dung. Nobody wants to smell that all through a church service.

All shapes and sizes of gray, brown, red, green, blue, and white frocks and tunics approached as other families came from the hills, responding to the church bell that echoed from the mountains. Arms were raised in greeting and "Hei Hei," called out faintly from far away and loudly from nearby.

We climbed the church steps and were greeted by an old gentleman in a black robe. "Welcome," he said to me from under bushy gray eyebrows. "You are a visitor?" he asked.

Agnas answered for me, "She is a friend visiting from Iceland for a while."

"Ah, so she came on your fishing boat, I hear," he replied.

"Ja. Runa and Runi met her part way," Agnas said, then she quickly turned to a woman and child coming up the steps, changing the subject. "Hei Hei. Did you have a good week?"

Runa took my elbow, "Let me show you something. Do you see the hole in the wall, there?" She pointed to a rectangle space. "In old days, those suffering from leprosy stood outside the church and listened to the sermon there. They also received the host through the hole."

When Fadir read the Bible, I heard about leprosy. The disease struck fear in a community as it spread and those afflicted lost fingers, toes, feet, hands, and even noses. The hole in the wall was a brilliant way for those who were contagious to still be included in worship.

Runa leaned in and continued in a low voice, "And whatever happened in Iceland – nobody needs to know. Just keep it to yourself." I nodded, set the food basket on a table and we slid in the pew by Agnas and Runi.

The preacher gave a sermon about Matthew 16:24: "Then said Jesus unto his disciples, If any man will come after me, let him deny himself, and take up his cross, and follow me." The preacher said that meant not just any man, but any woman or child, too. While the preacher droned on, I thought about what story I could tell about myself to conceal that I was a fugitive, and finally, a tale took hold in my mind.

CHAPTER 32

When the church service ended, people filed out and the volume of voices grew. Everyone wanted to get caught up with neighbors after a long week. Some smiling older ladies approached Agnas, "And who is this lovely young maid with you?"

This time I was ready with my own response, so when Agnas took a breath to answer, I quickly spoke, "I am Lara from Iceland. We heard from traders that the Faroese are clever, so my village sent me here to learn your ways. I hope to go to Norway to do the same there before returning to Iceland."

"Oh, my!" a woman wearing a red scarf exclaimed.

Another put her hand to her ample bosom. "You are a brave one."

Red scarf said, "We would like to visit more. Please join us for the meal."

"Takk," I said, "I think Runi and Runa are waiting for me." I smiled and backed away from the group.

I heard one of the ladies address Agnas, "She must be older than she looks."

"Ja. Maybe," said Agnas, smiling. "Did any of you get caught in the storm this week?"

I looked for Runa and Runi. Maids eager to share a meal with Runi surrounded him. "You are so brave and strong, Runi." "You can have your choice of food from my basket." "Are you going to the Althing next week?"

Runa sat a bit off to the side, and as I approached she rolled her eyes. "Is it always like this?" I asked her, chuckling.

"To be sure," Runa replied. "If I did not need him for the fishing so much, I would say marry already. The maids are knocking themselves out for him."

I laughed and a few heads turned toward us. I blushed and covered my mouth. "I thought that the lads were usually the ones to pursue the maids."

"Usually that is true, and especially here where the men outnumber the women by a good reckoning. But Runi is a fine catch, I have to admit. Even if he is my brodir." Runa took a bite of Skerpikjøt, a shank of dried mutton.

"What makes a man a good catch?" I asked.

Runa gazed out over the mountain and then began a slow list. "He must be hard-working … kind … truthful … gentle … strong … helpful. Oh, and clean."

"And handsome?" I asked.

"Only if he is all the other things first," Runa replied.

"Have you ever been in love?"

"I do not think so. Modir says I scare the lads off because I do not need a man. I can do nearly anything a man can do." Runa took another bite of the meat.

I said, "I have not been in love either. Modir and Fadir have said there is plenty of time for that, but some of my friends are moving toward marriage. I do not want to be left behind, but I also do not want to make a bad choice."

"Ja." Runa agreed. "I do not want a man like my fadir. I would rather be an old maid."

"Maybe we will be old maids together," I said, smiling.

"Maybe we will," Runa agreed.

CHAPTER 33

The week was filled with chores that were much the same as the week before. The main difference was all the excitement preparing to travel to the Althing in Torshavn.

I wanted to go, to see how it compared to the Althing in Iceland, but I was apprehensive, too. I felt more and more at home with Agnas' family, and I was reluctant to leave that security. We were getting into a routine of chores and Agnas relied on my help. Modir and Fadir would be proud to know that I was making myself useful. I did not commit to going to the Althing. Perhaps if I knew more of what to expect I would feel less apprehensive. I asked at supper, "How long does it take to get to Torshavn from here?"

Runa replied, "Oh, about a morning's walk. Not far, really. We will bring our own provisions to stay overnight." Runa replied. "And a few coins."

"In Iceland, the Althing is a big festival with booths and trading along with the parliamentary proceedings," I explained. "We spent months preparing things to trade."

"Was it far from your home?" asked Agnas.

"Ja. Many days' travel and some through dangerous barren lands."

"Faroe Island Althing is not so far and mostly about the law. Some trading is done, but we do not need anything. We have enough," said Runa.

I liked the idea of having enough and not wanting more. I thought of Edda and what her wanting got her. "Who is going?" I asked.

Runa looked at Runi, then to me. "Since our fadir is near, Runi will stay here with Modir."

Agnas objected, "No one needs to miss out on my account. Raven can stay." On hearing his name, Raven rose from his nap by the hearth and sat at Agnas' side. "See? He can help me." She patted Raven's head.

"I could stay," I offered. "I think the maids will be sad if Runi does not go." Agnas chuckled.

Runa said, "Runi went last year. You said you are good with a sling. I am good with a knife. We will be fine. We should go." She looked at me and nodded once, like that is that.

I felt like I was being pushed into going, and the last time I agreed to something Runa wanted me to do, I went fishing and nearly drowned. My lower lip poked out. Runa elbowed my arm and laughed. "We will have fun."

CHAPTER 34
TORSHAVN, FAROE ISLANDS ALTHING

Unlike the trek to Thingvellir from my home in Iceland, I put little thought into packing for this trip. Since we were only going to stay one night, mighty preparations were not necessary. The morning of our departure, I threw a few things in my pack. I left the Bible, fishing net, and waterproof cape on my badsofa. But I did pack my sling and also Birgir's special carved Vegvisir. After all, I did arrive here safely while carrying it. Raven was underfoot, hoping to join me on an adventure. He put his paw on my pack and looked up expectantly. "Not this time, Raven," I scratched behind his ears. I could see the disappointment in his eyes. "Agnas needs you." At the mention of Agnas, Raven went to her side and sat obediently.

Agnas wrapped some dried fish, mutton, and bread, and filled a canteen with fresh water. She tucked it all into my pack. "You carry this." Then she put her hand on my arm and whispered, "Hildur came to me in a dream last night. She will watch out for you and Runa."

Before I could respond, Runa entered the hut in a rush, her cheeks flushed and eyes bright. "Here's the tent and two blankets. I can carry these if you carry the food."

Agnas chuckled, "We have the same mind, Runa. Lara already has the food."

"Takk, Modir. Lara, are you ready?"

"Ja. I think so." I looked around the hut and patted my pack. I hoped I had what we needed for the trip.

When we opened the hut door, Runi was waiting outside. He gave Runa a small carved fish and he gave me a carved dog. "To bring you luck. If you want to trade it at the Thing, I will make you another one." I was touched at his thoughtfulness and impulsively reached up and hugged him. He returned the hug, holding on. I patted his back, and he let go. He slapped Runa on the shoulder. "Safe travels," he said, his voice husky.

"Come on, Lara," Runa said. I looked back at Runi and he raised his hand. His hair was shinier, his shoulders broader, and his eyes were brighter and bluer than I had noticed before. I remembered that Agnas spoke of how handsome he was and I thought about how the maids at the church picnic flocked around him like sheep to fodder. He really was handsome. Suddenly I was sorry he was not joining us.

CHAPTER 35

Runa set a fast pace and we trekked up a rocky hill surrounded by meandering, unperturbed sheep with brown, gray, white and spotted fleece. "Do the Faroese notch sheeps' ears to show who they belong to? That's what we do in Iceland."

"Ja. See those two with the small triangle missing from the lower left ear? They belong to us." Once she pointed them out, I could easily pick them out from the rest of the flock. "They are not far from home and will hear the bellwether when it is time for milking. Raven already knows which sheep are ours."

"He is a smart dog and a good companion."

"We had a sheepdog until two years ago. Modir loved that dog."

"What happened to him?" I asked.

"Fadir beat him to death with a rock when he would not stop barking one night. In the morning we found a dead, dismembered lamb. The dog was barking to warn about a predator, but he was another victim of Fadir's temper." I did not know what to say about such a disturbing revelation. We continued on in silence until we came upon an old abandoned drying shed that stood alone without a house to keep it company.

"Come with me," Runa said. I followed her into the shed and she opened her pack. She rummaged around and then pulled out lads' trousers, tunic, and belt like the clothes she wore. "I brought these for you. Put them on and put your maid's clothes in your pack."

"Why?"

"You will see. The Faroese Althing is attended mostly by men; you will feel less conspicuous dressing as they do. Changing here, Modir will not know. She barely tolerates that I dress this way." She pushed the trousers into my hands. "You will like it."

I had never worn lads' clothing. I felt the same excitement that I knew when dressing up in fancy clothes for church. I quickly changed. It felt strange to have the trousers separating my legs, but not in a bad way. When I cinched the belt, I looked up and saw that Runa had painted her face with black pointed eyebrows and some gray swirls and dots on her forehead and cheeks. "Runa!" I exclaimed in surprise, "You look fierce. And quite wonderful."

Runa smiled. "Do you want me to paint your face for you?"

I thought for a bit and then I said, "I think wearing lads' clothing is enough change for today. Maybe tomorrow?"

Runa nodded. "Tuck your sling in your belt. See? Like I have my knife." I did as she said. "There! Now we are proper Norsemen going to the Thing."

We again shouldered our packs and continued on our way. The walk was not difficult and we arrived well before our mid-day meal. As we approached the Torshavn harbor, I saw large ships anchored and a crowd of people milling among the buildings that were situated closed together and painted red or black with white around the doors and windows. The well-maintained sod roofs had sprinkles of tiny yellow and white flowers on them. The stone streets were worn smooth all the way out to a point in the harbor. "That is where the Law speaker will make pronouncements. And over there," she pointed to a hill behind the houses, "Is Gallows Hill where guilty men are hanged."

I felt a jolt in my chest. I was not sure I wanted to witness any more deaths. "Do I have to watch it all?"

"You can avoid whatever you want to," Runa reassured me. She turned when she heard her name called. "Come. I will introduce you to my friends."

A group of young men were standing nearby. One was waving to Runa. "Hei. Hei. Is Runi with you?"

"Nei. He stayed with Modir. But I brought Lara from Iceland. She is visiting."

"Welcome, Lara." The group of lads made space for us in their circle. Then they behaved as if I were not there. I was glad not to have to make conversation about myself. Runa was right. The lads' clothing made me feel like I blended in.

A bellwether wandered into the circle, acting confused about his whereabouts. One of the lads said, "Poor old man. He does not know if he is looking for a ram or a ewe, having lost his male parts so long ago." The rest of the lads laughed and nodded at each other with knowing glances.

"Maybe I need a bell," one of the others said, then he was quick to add, "but not the castration." All the lads laughed. "I meant to attract a fine ewe. I mean maid." The lads roared.

"Come, Lara," Runa said. "I am thirsty and I wager you are, too."

She produced some coins and approached a booth with drinking horns. "Two ales. And fill the horns to the top. No skimping." The very full horns were passed to us in exchange for the coins. "Drink up, Lara," she said.

"I have never had ale before," I said.

"Then you have been missing a great joy of life. You may not want to drink it too quickly, though. Pace yourself." At that, Runa took some big gulps. When she took the horn from her lip, it had foam on it. She licked all around her mouth. "Ahhhhh!" she sighed with a grin, "That is good."

I sipped from my horn. The ale tasted bitter and sour. I was not sure I liked the taste, but I loved the little bubbles that burst in my mouth. I took another sip. Then a larger swallow. I felt air rising and before I could stop it, a loud belch came from deep inside. I covered my mouth and could feel my neck and cheeks flushing. Runa slapped me on the back, "There you go! That is how it is done. You are a natural ale drinker." She planted her feet, made a strange face, and let out a loud belch. "See?" she said, "I told you we would have fun."

We sauntered among the people, and Runa commented all the way. She knew some local gossip and the ale seemed to have loosened her tongue. I could hear her, but I could not listen well. My head felt fuzzy, like it was full of wool. I tripped on a loose rock and Runa caught my arm. "We will sit for a while. I will find a place where we can see the logmadur and hear him recite the laws." She led me to a flat boulder near the Law Rock and I drowsily emptied my drinking horn.

When I woke up, I lifted my head and saw that I had drooled on Runa's shoulder. Embarrassed, I tried to wipe it off. Runa laughed and pushed my hand away, "You may be glad to know that you slept through the Law Speaker and the hangings."

I sat up in alarm. How could I have slept? We just got here. I shook my head and rubbed my eyes. Then I remembered the ale. And the story Fadir told of the man who lost a limb to frostbite after a long wander and sleep in the snow. The man must have had too much ale. Runa was teaching me about more than wearing men's clothing. My mind was divided about missing the Althing proceedings. I wanted to learn the Faroese ways, but not witnessing more deaths was a relief. My belly growled.

"You are hungry. While you slept, I got some food and water from your pack. Here. You will feel more awake after you eat and drink some water." She pushed a bundle onto my lap and I eagerly drank from the canteen and then ate my fill of fish and bread. "Drink more water," she encouraged, "And then we will explore." I did as she said. Then we grabbed our packs, and stood. I was stiff from sleeping on the hard rock, but walking limbered me. While I slept, Runa must have made a hole in the wooden fish Runi carved for her. I saw that she now wore it on a leather strap around her neck. I felt the pendant Modir gave me. The silver was warm against my skin.

We went to the harbor area and there, to my surprise, I saw the same merchant who I bought spices from at Iceland's Thingvellir. As we passed his table, he flashed his bright smile and called, "Come. See. Smell. Taste," just has he had at Thingvellir. We passed by without stopping. I do not think he remembered me. It was strange to think that I saw him less than a full moon phase ago.

Runa had her sights on a table with finely crafted blades. She picked them up one by one to examine them, plucking at each sharp edge with her thumb. "This one," she held one out to the merchant. "Will you take my blade and a leg of mutton in trade?" She held out the knife from her belt. The merchant, a bald, wizened man with tufts of white hair sprouting from his ears and nose pursed his lips as he pondered her offer. When he opened his mouth, I saw that he had only one tooth on the top and two on the bottom.

"I should not say Ja," he said in a slow, raspy voice, "But you will be my first sale of the day and that is good luck. And I am hungry. So," he paused dramatically, "I do say Ja." Runa handed him her old blade and held out her hand to me. I retrieved the leg of mutton from my pack. The man took it with his claw-like hand and Runa slipped her new blade into her belt.

"A sharp blade is necessary for my work." she looked around. "I just traded our supper. We will get our food another way."

Runa approached a circle of men who were throwing two square bones with dots on them on the ground. She held out the new blade she had just acquired. "I will wager this blade for two legs of mutton that the next roll will be doubles," she called out. I did not know what she was talking about or what they were doing.

"Done!" shouted a man in a fine suit of clothes.

"You have the mutton here?" Runa asked. "I showed you my blade. You show me the mutton."

He reached into a pack at his feet and produced two large legs of mutton that looked to be properly fermented and dried in the Faroese way.

"Roll then," Runa commanded. The man shook the bones between his cupped palms and blew onto them before tossing them into the circle. "Ha!" Runa said, "Two threes. Pay up."

Reluctantly, the man handed over the meat while the other men guffawed at his expense. "Outsmarted by a mere maid, " one man said.

Another replied, "That is no ordinary maid. That is Runa."

(HAPTER 36

We heard a deep cough and then a loud voice behind us. "Dottir. You have something for your fadir?" We turned to see big Johan standing with his hands on his hips, feet spread and planted.

"Nei. I have nothing for you," Runa looked at him with defiant eyes. She quickly stuffed the mutton in her pack. Johan reached out and fingered the carved fish Runa wore around her neck. She slapped his hand away and said gruffly, "Let us pass." Runa took my hand and tried to go around Johan. He stepped in front of her and blocked her way. I sensed movement behind us; the men interrupted their game to stand behind Runa and me.

Johan's eyes rose above us to the men. "Nothing to see here," he held out his hands in supplication.

Two of the men took a step in his direction. One spoke in a gruff voice, "Move along, Johan. You are not welcome here." Then I knew that he was not only hated by his family, but by these men, too. Runa quickly led me away. Her hand trembled in mine.

"He frightens me," I said. "He frightens you, too."

"He angers me to the point that I feel that I cannot control myself. If the men had not stepped in, I may have put my new blade to good use," she confessed. "If I thought Modir would forgive me, I would have done away with him long ago."

At that moment, I desperately missed my own kind and dear fadir. Before leaving home, I had never thought that others might not be so blessed. Now I know that there are bad, even evil fadirs in the world. If Pjetur had lived, he may have been that kind of fadir. Being an orphan, Edda did not know the love of a good fadir. And now her baby would not have a fadir either. I was not sure if I felt guilty or proud about that. I turned to see where Johan had gone and saw him rowing a tender to an anchored ship far out in the bay. I hoped he would stay on the ship all night so that Runa and I could enjoy our time here.

I heard shouting from the shoreline and men scrambling to get in small fishing boats. Runa said one word, "Whales." We stood on a high outcropping of rocks and watched fishermen row out into the harbor, near the breakwater, then form a circle. The boats then slowly began to row back to shore, closing the gaps between them. The water in the circle of boats churned and I saw black fins appear and disappear in the waves. Another group of men waded from the shore toward the pod of whales with large knives raised. When the whales were trapped in a tight group. Men jumped from the boats and joined the men from the shore with knives drawn. They all converged on the whales, slicing and stabbing. Blood from the whales spread until the bay and the rocky shore were red. The huge fish were pushed and pulled onto the shore where others joined in the butchering. I was both fascinated and horrified. Runa said, "I see that the blood has drained from your face, just like the blood is drained from the whales. You have never seen a whale hunt before?" I shook my head. "It is a necessary tradition for our survival. We are lucky that so many men were here to help. " She shrugged. "The people must live." I nodded numbly. Yes, I thought, we must live.

CHAPTER 37

After the whale hunt, the meat and blubber were parceled out and left cooling in the water until each person attending the Althing could take a portion home the next day. The men who did the slaughtering and butchering swam in a clean part of the bay and emerged with wet, but cleaner clothing. They sat on rocks and drank ale while waiting for their clothing to dry and their voices got louder and louder.

Runa and I set up our tent and ate our mutton, then joined others around a big fire as the sky grew dim. Tales of sea voyages and legends of trolls were interrupted with singing and laughter until yawns overtook us and one by one, the gathering thinned when folks drifted off to sleep. We spread out our blankets and crawled under our tent. Runa's sleepy voice was rumbly and low, "So, Lara. How was your day?"

I thought for a minute. "Good."

"And we had fun, did we not?" she asked.

"Just as you promised," I assured her. She rolled away and snuggled under her blanket. I did the same. "Good sleep, Runa."

"Um hum," she replied, and soon I heard her deep, rhythmic breathing. I also heard muffled voices of a few of the folks still gathered at the fire. The last sounds I remember of that night were calls of, "Good sleep to you." " Pleasant dreams." " See you in the morning." I held the wooden dog Runi carved for me as I drifted off to sleep. I dreamed of beautiful swimming and leaping whales.

With the arrival of morning light, folks wandered around, gathering their packs, eyes squinting and heads aching from the ale of the night before. Runa woke energetic and ready to go, just like on early fishing days. "We will claim our share of the whale and get back home to hang it to dry before the sun gets high and warm." When we got to the water's edge, I was relieved to see that the ship that Johan was traveling on was no longer in the harbor; it must have sailed in the night. The whale meat and blubber had been cooling in the water, so when we lifted our packages, they were wet. We shouldered our packs and the whale meat and said our farewells to fellow travelers as we headed through town and toward the hills that led back to Agnas, Runi, and Raven. The back of my clothing quickly became wet and oily and a powerful fishy odor rose from the whale. I was glad that I was not wearing my own clothing, but when we reached the same abandoned drying shed where we had changed on our way to the Althing, Runa said, "Here we are. Time to change back into your shift and apron." Seeing the look on my face, she laughed, "Do not worry. Modir knows how to wash clothes that seem spoiled by oily fish. And she will be happy to see you in your own clothes, not mine."

While I changed, Runa wiped off her fierce face paint. I had never known a woman who was so fierce and brave. And I was honored that she wanted me to go to the Thing with her. From now on, if she told me that we would have fun, I would believe her.

CHAPTER 38
KIRKJUBOUR FAROE ISLANDS

When we reached the top of the foothills, white birds swooped and dived and then disappeared into clefts of the mountain. "They are nesting," Runa remarked, shielding her brow with her hand. "Another day, we will gather eggs. They are a nice change from fish and mutton. Modir can use them in baking, too. Some of the neighbors keep geese and we can also trade for their big eggs."

"I know I have seen these places before, but things look different somehow. I feel like we have been gone a long time, even though our trip was only overnight. Maybe that is because we saw and did so many things." I said.

"Maybe...." Runa replied. "Being away from home always feels long to me." That surprised me. Runa seemed so adventurous and confident, but I wondered if she was brave because she felt so secure at home with Agnas and Runi. Maybe that is why I have been able to adjust to my changing circumstances, too. Fadir and Modir were good and loving to me. Oh, how I missed them and wondered how they fared.

Soon we saw the top of St. Olav Church and then the farms and houses of our valley home. When we got closer, I saw Runi milking sheep in the yard. Raven spotted us first and began to bark and jump with his tail waging like a flag in a storm. Then he broke into a run, galloping like a horse being chased by a wolf until he reached us. He jumped up on me, then on Runa with his tongue out and a big toothy smile. He sniffed the packs on our backs. Runi stood and raised his hand. "Hei Hei, travelers!" he called. Agnas emerged from the hut, wiping her hands on her apron and waving them both at us.

Runa took big strides ahead of me and slapped Runi's back. I followed with Raven. Runi began to reach out to me, then suddenly bent to pat Raven's head instead . "Come in! Come in!" Agnas said, "I want to hear all about it!"

Runa said, "First we need to process this whale meat and blubber and wash up."

Runi replied, "Oh! I missed a grindadrap?" He could not hide his disappointment.

"Ja. Big one. Whale meat for everyone." Runa said.

All four of us helped slice the meat and blubber, dredging the pieces in salt before hanging them in the drying shed. The work went quickly. Agnas fetched clean clothes for us and we bathed in the cold spring. Agnas set our smelly, greasy clothes to soak in a urine and water mixture and then we all went in the hut to for our mid day meal: Agnas' freshly baked bread and warm stew. We gathered around the table, and before we ate, I asked if I could say a prayer. Everyone set down their spoons and waited. "It is a traditional Norwegian prayer that my modir taught me." I cleared my throat and sang, "In Jesus' name to the table we go / To eat and drink according to His word / To God the honor, us the gain / So we have food in Jesus' name. Amen."

A chorus of "Amens" went around the table. "Beautiful," Runi said, his eyes shining.

Agnas beamed while we told her of all of our adventures, even the part about her scoundrel husband. Her pride in Runa was only surpassed by her love. Every part of her countenance shown like the sun when she looked at her children.

Agnas told of Runi's work on the fishing boat, making some needed repairs using driftwood they had been saving. She continued, "You two maids may rest a bit after your travels, if you like, but then the rest of the sheep need to be milked and skyr, butter, and cheese started yet today."

Runa yawned loudly, then winked at me. "I am so tired. Are you tired, Lara?"

"Maybe a little. But I can start the milking." I offered. Runa nudged my foot under the table and gave me a stern look. "Or maybe a short nap first."

"I will clean up and wake you after a while," Agnas offered.

Runi snorted, "They are only trying to get out of work," he said.

"Go on, now, Runi," Agnas said, "You can go to bed early tonight."

Runa chuckled as she crawled into her badsofa. I had to admit, the clean, soft blanket, quiet badsofa cubicle, and homey aroma of baked bread made my eyelids heavy and I fell asleep in an instant. I once again dreamed of Hildur, Modir, Fadir, and Ole singing an unfamiliar but comforting tune together. When Agnas opened my badsofa door, I reluctantly left them in my dream. The recurring dream reassured me that my family was safe. Or, at least I hoped they were.

CHAPTER 39

Through the rest of the summer months, the five of us, Agnas, Runa, Runi, Raven, and I fell into an easy routine of household chores, farming, fishing, attending church, and occasional longhouse gatherings with neighbors. A dance that autumn changed my life once again.

That mild and sunny autumn day, we stopped our chores mid-afternoon to get ready. I dressed in my best shift and belt – the one I made to go to Thingvellir. I plaited my hair and Runa's too and gathered small flowers into wreaths. Runa smiled when I showed her the wreath for her head. "I do not wear flowers," she said. "Maybe Modir would like it."

"Agnas, may I fix your hair?" I asked. She promptly sat on a chair and removed the scarf from her hair. Then she began to uncoil her wavy gray hair and I was astounded to see that it reached to the floor. Using my Bestemor's bone comb, I gently worked from the bottom fringes up to her scalp, untangling and then dividing, braiding and coiling the strands. Finally, I finished with the flower wreath.

"Are you done?" Agnas asked eagerly. When I said I was, she jumped up and went to the window to see her reflection. When she turned back to me, her eyes were wet. "Oh, I am a foolish old woman," she said, "But I do like to look nice. Thank you, dear Lara."

When it was time to walk down to the longhouse, Agnas gave the berry pie she had prepared to Runi to carry. Runa held Agnas' arm to steady her. I followed and admired my Faroese family. They were a handsome group, especially Runi. I found that my gaze often followed him since he hugged me so long before I left for Torshavn. But as much as I wanted to be near him, I felt a strange shyness when he was around. Our conversations centered on work tasks, and it seemed that we were both careful not to touch each other. When passing food at the table, our fingers grazed once and I felt like I had been pricked by a hot needle; it felt almost dangerous. Sometimes I would catch him looking at me, and then he would flush a deep red from his neck to his forehead. We had attended other dances that summer, but as usual, Runi was flocked by maids and our paths did not cross.

The windows and doors of the longhouse were open to let in cooling air, but it was warm inside anyway. High and low voices filled the air, interrupted by laughter. Fiddlers tuned their instruments, the drumbeats started, fiddles joined, and the dancing began. The preacher hovered around the table where Agnas and Runa worked with some of the other women setting out the food. I was going to join them when a hand reached my elbow. A squeaky male voice asked, "Will you dance with me?" I turned to see Alfrid, a boy with fuzz on his upper lip and the big feet and lanky look of a growing lad. He held out his hand, and I accepted. He valiantly but awkwardly held my hands in his sweaty palms and stepped on my feet more than once. "Sorry. Sorry," he nervously apologized over and over.

I smiled and gamely tried to follow his lead, but was relieved when that tune ended. "Thank you, Alfrid," I said, "I will go and help Agnas with the food now."

He backed away and bumped into a man holding a horn of ale. "Watch yourself," the man scolded. I felt sorry for Alfrid. In a few years, he would grow to be a fine man, I was sure.

On my way to the food table, I passed a circle of giggling maids batting their eyelashes at – of course – Runi. He saw me as I passed and gently pushed aside some of the maids. "Excuse me," he said. We met just as another tune began. Without a word, he gathered me in his arms and swept me out into the dancing crowd. I could hardly breathe. His strong embrace made me feel weak. I looked up at his flushed cheeks and shining eyes. He smiled and my heart felt like it was too big for my bodice. We fell into a relaxed rhythm as if we had danced together all our lives. I wanted to laugh but suddenly my voice caught and my sight grew blurry. I sighed and laid my head on Runi's chest. My flower crown fell and Runi caught it on his wrist without missing a step.

CHAPTER 40

After a couple more dances with Runi, he asked, "Are you thirsty? Hungry?"

"I am. Are you?" He smiled and took my hand, leading me to the food table. Agnas had her back to us; she was deep into a conversation with the Widow Ingaborg.

But Runa looked at us with a crooked grin and one eyebrow raised. "What is this, then? Are you two only dancing with each other tonight?"

Runi said, "Why? Do you want to dance with Lara? Or with me?"

I let the two of them trade words while I helped myself to some cold juice and a plate of cheese, meat, and of course – some of Agnas' berry pie. Seeing an empty spot on a nearby bench, I sat and began to eat. A married couple stood just as Runi and Runa came with full plates and took spots next to me. "I would like to ask what this means, the two of you together, but I am guessing you do not know yet yourselves. Am I right?" Runa shouted over the music.

Runi and I exchanged glances. Runi blushed and I shrugged. Runa was right; I had no idea what it all meant. I had never felt like this before. And, I had never talked with Runi about his thoughts and feelings. I did not feel any urgency to declare our intentions; I believed that things would happen as they should. So, I remained silent and Runi did the same.

Runa looked from me to Runi and back again. "Well?" When neither of us spoke, Runa became angry. "So you two form an alliance without me? I am to be left out?" She stood with her plate and stomped out the door. Runi and I looked at each other and, without a word between us, followed Runa outside.

Runa stood by the rocky shore where the gathering darkness was interrupted by a celestial spectacle. We approached her and, without turning around, Runa said, "Aurora." Looking northward we saw the brilliant, changing swirls of green, pink, and blue pulsing above us. None of us spoke. We finished eating our food while standing and gazing upward. The scene felt like a prayer. I perceived a faint hum in the air, like a quiet monk's chant that echoed in my chest. I had seen the aurora at home in Iceland during frosty nights, but tonight the lights seemed different somehow. As if reading my thoughts, Runa said, "It is a sign. Seeing you together tonight, I could not deny it any longer. I have known since we pulled Lara from the sea months ago." She paused. "You are meant to be together."

I looked at Runa with surprise, then at Runi. His eyes filled. "Ja, Runa. I felt it, too." Then he took my hand, "Lara, I have loved you from the first time I saw you and lifted you from the raft into our boat. I questioned myself many times; I tried to deny my feelings. You should seem like a sister to me, but this is the truth: you are my one true love."

I was caught off guard. Was my future to be decided by Runa and Runi? Suddenly, I felt that I was being pushed into something I had not seriously considered. I was of marrying age, having just passed my sixteenth year, but I wanted time to think and to examine my own heart. The need to escape overpowered me. I said, "I am very tired; I am going back to the hut." I handed my empty plate to Runa, turned, and left. On my way up the hill, I wondered what they were saying to each other.

CHAPTER 41

When I woke the next morning, and opened the door of my badsofa, the day was already begun. Agnas looked up from her mending, "Good morning. I hope you are feeling better. Runa and Runi said you were not feeling well when you left the dance last night, so we let you sleep."

I was a bit amused that they gave an excuse to their modir about my sudden exit, but maybe they were right. Perhaps I was not feeling well. If I were well, I would welcome Runi's profession of love. I certainly enjoyed being held while we danced. But it was all happening too quickly. It seems that Runa and Runi both got a special message about my destiny, but I did not. My head hurt and when I stood, the room swirled like last night's aurora.

"Steady there, " said Agnas. "A strong cup of tea and breakfast is what you need." She bustled to set the table. I began to eat and Agnas sat across the table from me and caught my eye. "I have a good listening ear," she said.

"Oh, Agnas," I said. "I have so much to think about."

Agnas nodded and sat quietly as I finished my food. She rose and poured herself a cup of tea and joined me again. We sipped in silence and then Agnas spoke. "I think I know why you are pensive." She whispered, "Hildur showed me a wedding in the church here."

My heart pounded. Agnas looked in my eyes and continued, "Do you want to know more?"

"I am not sure," I admitted. Raven put his head on my knee.

The sound of boots on gravel and a loud pounding on the hut door interrupted us. Raven barked and growled until I called to her to stop. Agnas opened the door to reveal two large men in tattered sailing garb, and in need of a bath. "Is this the hut of Runa Johansdottir?"

"Ja. I am Agnas, her modir."

"You are wife of Johan?"

"Ja. What is this about?"

"Our ship's captain sent us from Torshavn. We have news of Johan."

"Come in and sit." She turned to me, her face serious. "Lara, go get Runa and Runi from the drying shed." She went to the hearth to get food and drink for the visitors.

The men sat at the table with a grunt and a growl. I quickly fetched Runa and Runi who came without argument. Agnas put the food and tea before the men and we all sat. I breathed through my mouth; the stench coming from the men burned my nose. They slurped their stew and chewed noisily with open mouths, more interested in eating than in talking. We waited for them to finish, exchanging anxious glances among ourselves. Finally the one with the bushiest beard leaned back, belched, and rubbed his greasy waistcoat. "Ahhhh. Good." he proclaimed. "And now the news. Your husband and fadir Johan was killed in a knife fight in Norway. His killer has become a fugitive. Johan was buried just outside the churchyard. Since he was not a godly man, the church would not have him." The man picked his teeth with his fingernail and noisily sucked in air.

The other man took up the tale, "But we put a stone with a cross on his grave anyway." He nodded with pride. Then he winked at Runa. "You are the maid who can better a man. We have heard about you." Then he looked at Runi. "And you look strong, like your fadir in his youth. If you are a sailor, we can use you to replace your fadir on the ship." Raven paced between the door and my chair.

Agnas swayed in her chair and Runi jumped up just in time to catch her before she fell. Runa maintained a stony silence and an unperturbed face. Runi was most concerned with Agnas. "Modir!" He gently patted her cheek. "Modir! Lara, will you get fresh water?"

I grabbed the water bucket and ran to the stream and back as fast as I could, Raven on my heels. When I returned, Agnas was sitting on the floor, Runi supporting her shoulders. Raven licked her hand. Agnas muttered, "Hildur showed me his gravestone." I knelt and gave her a cup of water. She took a sip. "Hildur knows," she whispered. "She sees and she knows."

CHAPTER 42

The men rose to leave. The heavily bearded one turned back, "You coming with us, Lad?" he asked Runi.

Runi looked at Agnas, then at me, at Runa, and back to me. Runa was like a wooden doll, unmoving at the table. I did not respond. Runi turned. "Modir?" he asked.

Agnas held her chair and stood. "You are a grown man, Runi. Runa and Lara can help me here. If you feel the need to go, I give you my blessing."

Without hesitation, Runi said to the men, "Wait for me to pack; I will come." They stepped outside.

I stood and cleared the table and began the washing up, concentrating mightily on the work of my hands and not on what Runi was doing. Soon he said, "Farewell, Runa. Take care of Modir." He hugged Agnas and kissed her cheek. "Farewell, Modir. I will come home when I can." Then he came to me. He swept me in his arms and kissed me on the lips. "Do not forget me, Lara. I will be back." With that, he left. I stared at the door. My mouth hung open and my hands dripped water.

CHAPTER 43

Our days were filled with work. Runi had always made fishing with Runa look so easy. Runa was abrupt with me; I could not seem to master the easy way she and Runi worked together. We all missed his quiet, assuring company. Agnas confided that they had never been apart for more than a day or two their whole lives. I worked hard to fill the gap left by Runi, and although I had I thought I was strong, my whole body ached after a day at sea. But the more I worked, I felt the muscles in my arms, legs, and back strengthen and I was less fearful of the sea. When we weren't fishing, we prepared for the coming winter months when freezing cold temperatures and ice and snow would keep us from outdoor tasks. Along with the supply of dried fish and meat, we stored potatoes under the hut floor. We gathered wheat for our bread and hay to sustain the sheep when snow covered the ground. My thoughts about Runi were tangled as a knotted skein of wool, and my heart felt dull and empty. Each night, I fell exhausted into my badsofa and, as I drifted into deep sleep, I held the wooden dog that Runi carved for me.

Agnas prayed loudly and fervently for Runi, often at surprising moments, like in the middle of sheep shearing or when working in the drying shed. Raven sat expectantly by Runi's badsofa or by the hut's door, waiting for him. Runa divided herself between silence and a smoldering anger. One day, after a hard morning at sea when I could not seem to anticipate anything she wanted, she finally snapped. "Could you not have returned Runi's declaration of love? If you had not left him wondering, he would not have gone away."

I was stunned. I thought only I blamed myself for Runi's departure. I felt guilty and ashamed. Did I love Runi? Would Modir and Fadir think he was a good match? How I wished I could talk to them. Did Modir feel like this about Fadir when they met back in Norway? Runi was a hard worker and kind. And I did think he was handsome – even more so as time went on. The longer he was away, the more I missed him – just as Agnas and Runa did. Agnas hoped he could get back to us before winter ice and storms prevented his ship from returning. As the days grew darker and colder, I searched the hills for his approach. When in the hut, I strained my ears for his footsteps. When I lay on my badsofa to sleep, I prayed for him. But as the first snowflakes of winter fell, so did my spirits. Would he return? Would he still love me? Might he have met another maid while he was away? Agnas and Runa were more quiet than usual. Separately, we held a silent, despairing vigil that became less and less hopeful of Runi's return. Whatever my hands were engaged in, my mind and heart concentrated on only him. I was rarely hungry, but ate out of habit and Agnas' urging. I had heard maids speak of "lovesickness" when working in the pit house at home. Was I lovesick? I began to believe it.

CHAPTER 44

On a gray, timeless morning after a hard frost the night before, I opened the hut door to let Raven out and nearly fainted. There stood Runi, bundled in layers of clothes and with a full beard. When he saw my surprise, his bright blue eyes twinkled and he laughed. "Lara, you look like you have seen a ghost."

"Runi!" I exclaimed.

Agnas and Runa hurried to the door and I backed away to observe their happy reunion. Agnas sobbed and hung on Runi's neck. Runa wore a big grin as she slapped his back and shoulders. Finally, Agnas pulled him inside the hut and closed the door. "Take off those clothes and put on clean ones. I will boil some water for you to have a quick bath. Are you hungry? Runa! Set the kettle on and Lara, get some stew and bread ready."

Runi just smiled and his cheeks grew rosy as they warmed. "Ja, Modir. A bath and some warm food would be good. The hike from Torshavn was windy and cold." Agnas handed him blankets to hang from the rafter beams to give him some privacy and he began to peel off layers of clothing. I felt a warm flush creep up my neck at the thought of Runi without clothes. He must have sensed my thoughts. He winked at me. I could not help but smile.

After he had changed, the four of us sat at the table while Runi ate. Raven paced around his chair until finally settling on top of his feet under the table. Between bites of food, Runi told us about the Dutch sailing ship built of Norwegian pine. On its outbound journey from the Faroes, the trading vessel brought with it wool and dried fish. When it arrived in the tropical Caribbean Islands, the ship picked up a cargo of people with skin as dark as a pilot whale. Runi said they were put in the cargo hold of the ship. Of the survivors, some were delivered to France, and some to England. Those who died of illness or injury during the voyage were thrown into the sea. Runi said, "I asked why the people were kept below deck. The older sailors said that they were not really human, but I did not believe that. Some of the women gave birth on the ship and their babies cried just like ours do. I heard singing and talking, just like what we do. But my objections were quickly squashed by the other sailors." He paused to take a bite of bread. "The money is good, but still…." We waited while he ate some more. "Once the cargo hold was emptied of the people, the ship was loaded with fabrics, ale, wine, spirits, spices, tea, coffee, and grains that passed between France and England. Then goods were brought to Norway. In the port of Bergen, the Hanseatic League bartered for goods on the ship. From Norway, we brought bog iron and lumber here. The ship will continue to Iceland if the weather holds."

"What a grand adventure you have had, Runi," said Agnas. "Now you may be settled to stay home for a while."

"I will stay through the winter. After that, I am not certain." His eyes held mine.

My mind was stuck on the word Norway. "I have family in Norway. I would like to go there." Perhaps I could finish my three-year banishment and know my Norwegian family, too.

Runi regarded me with a solemn expression. Then he rose and knelt by me. "Lara, if you will marry me, I promise I will take you to Norway."

I felt the rest of the hut fall away as I looked into his eyes. "Yes," I said. "Dear Runi, I will marry you."

Agnas jumped up and clapped her hands. Runa rose and fetched a hidden bottle of spirits. "This calls for a celebration. I have a soster," she said.

Runi kissed my hand and held it. His large warm hand completely enveloped mine. "Skol!" they shouted as we drank from our cups. I felt the warm liquid coursing down my throat to join the warmth in my heart. Now that the decision was made and declared, I could breathe again. And suddenly, I was hungry.

"May I have some of that stew?" I asked.

"Dottir, you may have all of it." I hungrily took a few bites. Agnas continued, "And I will go down the hill to speak to the preacher today. A wedding! How wonderful!" Runi kissed my hand again and then held it up until I stood with him. He folded me into his strong arms and this time I was not shy. I reached up and took his soft beard in my hands and kissed him. His passionate response weakened my knees. He smelled of soap and fresh air. I never wanted him to go away again.

CHAPTER 45

The yuletide season found us inside, furtively making gifts, often with our backs to the fire rather than facing each other. For the wedding, I would wear my Icelandic Althing frock with my arctic fox cape. I hung it from the rafters to ease the creases, and I wove some wheat and holly into a crown. Runi and I stole smiles and kisses, and when Runa and Agnas left to visit neighbors one afternoon, we shared his badsofa. I was nervous at first, but he was gentle and my body responded to his so that afterwards, I found myself looking forward to this pleasure as his wife. Our wedding was planned for December 26, Christmas the second. Since Agnas liked to feed friends and neighbors on that day anyway, we would have the wedding celebration at the church enjoying food that Agnas loved to prepare.

On Christmas Eve, our small family gathered for a mid day meal of fermented fish and we shared a bottle of berry wine. After our meal, we gathered at the hearth. I stood and said, "As one of my gifts to you, I will sing an Icelandic hymn I have known since I was a small child." I sang for them the ancient song, Heyr Himna Smidur. When I finished the last note and sat down, a hush had fallen over us. Agnas clasped her hands below her chin and Runa blinked and blinked. Runi reached over and squeezed my arm.

Finally, Agnas spoke, "My dottir, you could not have given us a more beautiful gift." She reached into her knitting basket and gave Runi a new woolen hat in a shade of bright blue that matched his eyes.

Runi immediately put it on and tilted his head from side to side. "Handsome, yes?" he teased. "Thank you, Modir."

Then she gave Runa and me matching gray and green striped hats and mittens, expertly knitted. Runa passed to each of us bags made by knotting the same cording that was used for the fishing nets. Runi smiled, "And you made me believe I was the only one who could tie knots to repair the fishing nets. Your secret is out now, Runa." I produced small woven coin pouches and Runi gave them each a coin to put in them. He then put a bundle on Agnas' lap. "This is for the family," he said shyly. Agnas carefully unwrapped the small carved wooden pieces: first a swaddled baby, and a kneeling woman and man.

Agnas' eyes shown. "A crèche of our own," she held the figures to her chest. "A treasure."

Then he handed me the final gift. I unwrapped a beautifully carved figure with wings. "An angel for my angel," he said. We assembled the figures on the shelf above the hearth and the soft golden light from the dying embers caught the faces of the wooden figures and the faces of my Faroese family.

CHAPTER 46

Christmas Day came and went. We did chores in preparation for the party the next day and then played in the snow, making a snowman and throwing snowballs for Raven to chase. That night, I climbed into my badsofa for the last time. After tomorrow's wedding, I would share Runi's badsofa. I lay awake, holding my wooden dog and I thought about how much my life had changed since I left home to go to Thingvellir. I wished that my Icelandic family and friends could attend the wedding. I wanted Modir and Fadir to meet Runi and also Agnas and Runa. I wondered how Kristin and Edda were doing. Would I ever see them again? Would Ole remember me? I imagined returning to Iceland with Runi, my husband. I felt a warmth pass through me as I drowsed to sleep. My husband. Runi.

The sun peeked out from the clouds for a while on our wedding day and we took that as a good sign. Although it was not stormy, I was thankful for my warm fur cape and felt like a princess wearing it and my woven crown. Runi was handsome and dignified in the black suit he borrowed from the preacher. In a festive mood, friends and neighbors arrived at the church carrying gifts and food. The preacher read in his sonorous solemn voice the Bible passage about love from I Corinthians 13 and then Runi and I repeated our vows to love and be true to one another, "until death parts us." After the ceremony and while the food was being set out, a local craftsman tattooed the third finger of each of our hands with a small, intricate chain. Runi went first, and he did not flinch, so I was surprised at the sting and burn of the needle. But once done, I loved it; the dark gray chain stood out on the redness of my skin. Wedding guests gathered around to admire our new markings of commitment.

Fiddles and drums started the dancing and the church grew warm with all the party activities. After we had visited with all the guests and had our fill of eating and dancing, Agnas took Runi and me aside and said, "Runa and I will be here for quite some time, cleaning up. If the two of you want to go back to the hut now, we will excuse you. The preacher offered to walk me and Runa home later." Then she winked and smiled broadly.

Runi went to the musicians and asked them to pause. He raised both hands to the waiting crowd and said, "Thank you all for helping to make this day special for Lara and me. We will take our leave now and see you again soon as husband and wife." Couples exchanged knowing glances and smiles. We waved, Runi took my arm, and we left the church to begin our married life.

CHAPTER 47

When spring finally arrived, Runi and I had become accustomed to each other. He began fishing with Runa as soon as the sea ice allowed and the process of drying fish began again in earnest. In the evenings, I would see him leaning back in his chair, staring at the ceiling. "Runi," I finally said one night, "Are you deep in thought?"

He set his chair down on all four legs and smiled at me. "I am deep in planning. Soon I will be ready to tell you."

The snow melted and the muddy fields began to dry with the spring winds and occasional sunshine. The men gathered to shear the ewes before the lambing began. The preacher always took the bags of wool to Torshavn with his horse and wagon, and this time, Runi quickly offered to go along. We watched the wagon loaded with bags of wool disappear over the crest of the hill. Agnas shook her head and said, "I do hope Runi can get whatever is bothering him talked out with the preacher. He seems distracted these days."

"Do you think … that he is dissatisfied with me?" I worried aloud.

Runa snorted, "Dissatisfied with you? Nei. One look at my brodir and I can tell you he is love sick as ever with you."

I nodded, unconvinced. I accompanied Runa in the fishing boat but all the while, I scanned the shore for Runi's return and finally Runa barked at me as if she were Raven seeing a stranger. "Watch what you are doing here, Lara. Fishing can be dangerous business if you do not pay attention." Chagrined at her admonishment, I kept my head down until we were returning to shore with our catch. Far off, I saw a horse and wagon approaching and felt great relief to know that Runi was returning. I had the nagging feeling that he wanted to go back to work on the trading ship, and I was afraid that he might not return from Torshavn that day.

"Hei Hei," he called and waved and the preacher waved, too. Runa and I arrived at the hut when the preacher dropped Runi off. "Takk for the ride," Runi looked at the preacher and patted the horse's rump. He lifted a large, heavy package from the wagon and held it under his arm.

"It was my pleasure, Runi. God speed with your plans." The preacher waved once again and proceeded down the hill to the parsonage.

"What plans?" Runa asked. She was always one to get right to the point.

Runi shook his head and smiled. "Let me help you hang your catch in the drying shed," he said. I was curious, too, and wanted to know his secret, but he said to me, "Lara, would you please go and help Modir inside? I will help Runa out here."

I had a feeling that Runi would confide in Runa and I felt jealous of their closeness. I was his wife, after all. He should confide in me before anyone else. I was fuming when I reluctantly went in the hut. Agnas was straining skyr and struggling with the weight of the cloth over the bowl. I held it for her. Agnas said, "Do not worry, dear Lara. Runi will talk to you when he is ready." How did Agnas know what I was thinking? We finished with the skyr and Runi and Runa came inside. Runi had the heavy package with him and he set it on the table. He began to slowly unwrap it. All eyes were on the mysterious package that clunked and rolled with each pull of the fabric wrapping. What appeared when it was open were two large hooks and pulleys with an iron wench mechanism, some heavy rope, and sturdy wooden poles. "What is it?" Agnas asked.

Runi looked at me when he answered. "I did not want to raise your hopes before I knew this was possible, Lara. I will install this on the fishing boat so that Runa can fish by herself while we are away; it will assist with lifting the heavy net from the water."

I looked at the table and back at Runi and suddenly I knew his plan. "We are going to Norway?" I asked.

"Ja. I talked to the ship's captain. He said the ship will return to Torshavn during the half moon time and then it will cross to Norway. If I work on the vessel, he will give us both passage without cost."

"Oh, Runi," I jumped into his arms. He picked me up and spun me around. When he set me back on my feet, I saw Agnas' crestfallen face. "Dear Agnas," I took both of her hands in mine. "You are our modir. We will return."

"But I may not see you again," Agnas' eyes filled.

"Surely that is not true," I insisted.

"Only Jesus and Hildur know for sure," Agnas replied.

"Modir!" Runa said, "You and your spooky premonitions. All will be fine."

"Ja," Agnas said with a weak smile, "All will be fine."

CHAPTER 48

Runi spent the next days working on the hoist for the fishing boat. He and Runa tried out the net-lifter and made adjustments. With flushed cheeks, Runa reported on their progress at our mid day meal, "So, I can do it. Runi has set it up so that the fish fairly put themselves in the boat." I saw that Runa had tears in her eyes and realized how brave and cheerful she was about our departure. The idea of losing Runi, even for a short time, must have felt like losing an arm. Once again, I admired Runa's strength and her fierce love for her family. My eyes welled, too.

While Runa and Runi perfected the fishing gear, I worked in the fields, because the lambing had begun. Each lamb and ewe needed to be put in the pen to be safe from predators until weaning. As soon as I opened the hut's door in the morning, Raven ran out like a shot from a sling, eager to help me search for newly born lambs. The ewes could be secretive about giving birth, but Raven could sniff them out, and I felt like I had discovered treasure each time I heard the tiny newborn bleats. Usually there was only one lamb, but sometimes there were twins. I loved snuggling their soft bodies and nuzzling their pink noses while carrying them to the pen. Raven accompanied their mothers as they trotted along, following me and bleating loudly. I imagined I was being scolded for stealing the babies.

When not in the fields, I was in the hut, helping Agnas with chores and packing for our trip. I included the things I brought from Iceland, along with the hat and mittens that Agnas knit for me, and the carved dog from Runi. The dog's wooden surface was smooth and dark where I held it. When I came upon the sling that Fadir gave me, I became wistful for home and apprehensive about the sea voyage. Such mixed feelings. I was eager to kmow my Norwegian family, but afraid to leave the security of my home here. I fingered my silver pendant and thought about meeting its maker in Trondheim. I shook my head to return to the task at hand. What didn't fit in my old pack, I put into the bag that Runa gave me for Christmas. I left the angel Runi carved for me with the rest of the nativity figures to watch over Agnas and Runa in our absence. Runi sorted and packed his belongings the evening before our departure. That night, the last together in our badsofa, he whispered his urgent desire for me, and I eagerly responded.

CHAPTER 49
TORSHAVN FAROE ISLANDS

Early the next morning, Raven barked at the hut door. Runi opened it to find the preacher outside. "I knew this was your day to depart. I will take you and Lara to Torshavn in my wagon."

"Come in. Come in," Agnas called. She immediately set the table for breakfast.

The preacher joined us. "Agnas," he said, "This food is delicious. I hope that, in Runi and Lara's absence, you will be inclined to reach out to me when you need help." He paused and smiled, "And if you have any extra meals you need to have eaten."

Runa looked at Runi and me and lifted an eyebrow. I wondered at this development, too. Did the preacher have designs on the Agnas' affection? Perhaps our departure would open the way for new developments.

We finished eating and Runi and I made last-minute preparations while the preacher admired Runi's nativity carvings and examined the sweater that Agnas was knitting. "This will be a warm garment for a blessed person," he said. Runa cleared her throat loudly and our smiling eyes met.

Runi brought our packs out to the wagon and returned. "Modir," he said, taking Agnas in his arms, "We must leave now."

Agnas rested her head on Runi's chest, then stood on her toes and kissed his cheek. "Take care of yourself, and Lara, too," she said. Then she reached out for me and we embraced. "I will pray for you."

Runi then turned to Runa. He poked at the fish pendant she still wore. "Do not forget us, Runa. Take good care of Modir." He put his hands on both of her shoulders and kissed her cheek.

Runa nodded and came to me with a lopsided grin. I held her tightly. "Come back," she whispered.

The preacher put on his hat and opened the door. "After you," he said. I climbed onto the wagon seat and Runi got in the back of the wagon by our packs. The preacher patted Agnas on the arm, "I will be seeing you soon," he said. Then he climbed onto the seat next to me, clucked to the horse, and we were on our way.

CHAPTER 50
THE NORTH SEA

The ship was anchored out in the harbor, the same ship I saw Johan going to during the summer Althing. We said our farewells to the preacher and approached a dinghy to be taken to the ship. For a coin, the sailor rowed with well-muscled arms and a few grunts until we reached the ship. Runi climbed up the net ladder, shouldering our packs and I followed, doing my best to tuck my skirt between my legs and wishing I were wearing Runa's men's trousers and tunic. The sailor made no attempt to avert his gaze.

Runi showed me around the ship and introduced me to the captain. He was a weathered, bearded man with icy blue eyes that looked like he tolerated no nonsense. "While your husband is manning the ropes and working on deck, you will work in the galley."

"Oh, I did not know you would need my help."

"Hell," the captain said, "Not just your help. You are it. My last cook abandoned ship at our last port. I may be able to get a lad to assist you from time to time." He looked at me with those piercing eyes, "But you may prefer to work alone, if you catch my meaning."

That is how I became a galley cook on a merchant ship. Runi and I had brought some of our own provisions, which I concealed in a wooden drum in the galley, but the ship's captain and skeleton crew of nine other men would need to be fed. I surveyed the cramped kitchen and found it dirty and airless. I opened a hatch to let in fresh air, got a clean water bucket and lye soap and scrubbed every surface and every pot and utensil until the rotten stench was gone. When Runi came below to check on me, I was sweaty and disheveled. He tried to look concerned, but he burst out laughing. "You look like a proper galley maid," he teased. "I will get a kerchief for your hair."

I called after him, "I did not agree to this part of the deal." I did not have long to pity myself. It would soon be time for the mid day meal. I quickly peeled potatoes and set them to boil, then inventoried the remaining provisions, dividing them out to last until we arrived in Norway. If all went well, we would moor in Bergen, Norway in three days. I could do anything for three days.

A clamor of boots above and then on the steps alerted me that the men were ready for food. They noisily entered the galley, grabbing a plate on the way in and forming a makeshift line in the cramped quarters. The first in line held out his plate to me and I obligingly put a helping of potatoes and butter on it. "You are not the mangy dog who was cooking for us before. Who might you be, pretty maid?"

Runi, further back in the line, answered in a deep gruff voice I rarely heard from him, "She is my wife, working here for safe passage. Notice I said safe passage. She is not to be nettled."

A chorus of men's voices rose loudly, "Ooooooohhhhh. Tough lad defends his bride. Aye, then matey. We will leave your lovely lass be."

When Runi reached me with his plate, he passed me my apron and kerchief. I leaned in and whispered, "We will eat from our provisions later tonight." Runi winked and went with the others to eat. After I did the washing up, I went to the quarters that Runi and I would share. It adjoined the galley and was equally squalid. I took the blankets from the bed and found them full of vermin. I threw them all out the porthole into the sea and furiously scrubbed every inch of the quarters, ridding it of rat droppings, bugs, and dirt. Then I retrieved our packs and used our clean blankets to re-make the bed. I sprinkled herbs around the perimeter of the room to deter new pests and then it was time to make supper. The men were less talkative in line, no doubt as tired as I was, readying the ship to sail. While washing up after the meal, I heard the heavy chain clanking while the anchor was being pulled up. I went on deck where the sails rose and billowed, catching the early evening wind. Apparently, the captain felt confident to sail at night with the sun hardly setting. The captain's eyes surveyed the deck and lingered when he saw me. All of the men were working, pulling on ropes, calling orders to each other. I caught sight of Runi, his shirt off and muscles rippling as he grappled with a rope. Although I was tired and dirty, I could hardly wait until I could get cleaned up and he could join me in our freshly cleaned and cozy quarters where I would have him all to myself.

CHAPTER 51

I had never been on a big ship and I was pleasantly surprised to find that my earlier fears of the sea were unfounded. The gentle rolling of the waves and the quiet of our quarters were conducive to lovemaking and soothing for sleep. Since Runi was working for our passage and not as a paid crew member, he did not have to take a night shift, so he joined me in our cabin each night where we enjoyed the bread, dried fish, and mutton that we brought on board with us. I read to him from the Bible Kristin gave me until we could restrain ourselves no longer and fell into each other's arms. In later times, I would think on this time with Runi and long for those nights to return.

On our last day of the voyage, the captain came down to the galley while I was preparing supper. "You got along without help, I see," he began. "And your husband is satisfying your needs?" He looked me up and down and licked his lips. I felt a jolt of alarm and looked to the stairway, willing Runi – or anyone -- to interrupt him. The captain moved toward me and I backed up. He continued until I was in the doorway of the cabin Runi and I shared. He leaned in over my shoulder and sniffed. "Your quarters smell of musk." My heart was beating so hard I could hear it in my ears. Then I heard Fadir's steady voice in my head, "A well-placed knee…." I swung my leg and struck with force between the captain's legs. He doubled over and fell to the floor. I jumped over him and climbed the steps, tripping over my skirt. I reached the top on my hands and knees and paused to catch my breath. I looked up and saw Runi approaching. I had to make a decision. If I told Runi what happened, he would feel a need to defend my honor by challenging the captain. But we were nearly at our destination and we needed the captain to get there.

"What happened?" Runi asked. "You look like you have seen a ghost."

I laughed half-heartedly. "I just felt a bit sea sick and came on deck for fresh air."

Runi helped me up. He looked skeptical. "Sea sick? You have been fine until now." The captain emerged on deck from the galley steps and Runi looked at him and back at me. "Are you sure you are all right?"

"I am sure. I will finish preparing supper now." I gave the captain a hard look as I passed. He hung his head and limped to the bridge. I saw Runi watch him go, and figured I had not fooled him, but he did not pursue the captain. I straightened my apron, tidied my hair under my kerchief, and went downstairs.

CHAPTER 52

That night, while we ate the remainder of our provisions in our cabin, Runi said, "I think something more happened today than what you told me. I also think that you handled it. I will not pressure you to tell me, but if you want to tell me now, or later, I would be grateful."

I thought about what he said. He would be grateful? To be taken into my confidence? I was tempted to bare my soul to Runi about the captain and about what happened to Pjetur in Iceland. But something held my tongue, and instead I kissed him and said that I was tired and wanted to sleep. He put his arm around me and we snuggled in. Soon I heard his soft snoring, but my mind would not be stilled. I expected Runi to confide in me, but I was not willing to confide in him? Would he still love me if he knew I was a fugitive? And one other thing: I had not had my bleeding for two moon cycles. Someday I would tell him about killing Pjetur, the captain's rude advances, and that I may be with child, but this was not that day.

I was nearly asleep when I heard shouting from the deck. I shook Runi awake and we went topside to see what the commotion was about. A sailor in the crow's nest at the top of the mast was shouting: "Ahoy! Land!" Lights blinked in the distance and large white birds circled the ship, a sure indicator of approaching land. Sailors appeared at each deck station and Runi took his post as well. He had explained to me that coming into a harbor was one of the most dangerous parts of a voyage. The ship could too easily be thrust into shoals and rocks, and many have sunk within sight of land. The captain's expertise was imperative. I listened as the captain called out commands and the men responded. The ship threaded its way through increasingly shallow water toward the harbor. In the light of the midnight sun, I saw the black fins of whales riding the wake of the ship. We were approaching the land of my people. The shouts of the seamen receded and I recalled a song that Modir sang in Norwegian before holiday meals. I sang it softly to myself:

> "Be present at our table, Lord;
> Be here and everywhere adored;
> Thy creatures bless, and grant that we
> May feast in paradise with Thee.
>
> We thank Thee, Lord, for this our food,
> For life and health and every good;
> By Thine own hand may we be fed;
> Give us each day our daily bread.
>
> We thank Thee, Lord, for this our good,
> But more because of Jesus' blood;
> Let manna to our souls be giv'n,
> The Bread of Life sent down from Heav'n."

My heart felt like it would burst with gratitude – to Modir and Fadir, to my friends in Iceland, to Runi, Runa, and Agnas, to Odin, to Hildur, to Jesus. They have brought me this far, and they will bring me home.

CHAPTER 53

BERGEN NORWAY

A row of colorful buildings lined Bergen's pier. The deep harbor allowed ships to be tethered alongside the wharf where cargo was being loaded and unloaded. Wagons full of goods lined the walkway. The noise of people and animals was nearly deafening after the hushed sounds of the ship at sea. I quickly packed up all of our things and righted the galley for the next cook. I left the bed in our cabin bare, having tossed the old bedding overboard, but I reckoned the captain could pay for his behavior and my silence by restocking the quarters. Runi appeared to help me carry the packs and we walked together down the gangplank. Now that we had arrived, Runi said he felt no compulsion to continue to work. I saw the other sailors unloading bags of wool from the ship; they may have been the very bags of wool that Runi and the preacher delivered to Torshavn. A couple of the sailors appeared lazy, working in slow motion. I hoped, in fairness to the others, that they would pull their weight; they all had a full day of lifting ahead of them. Loads of lumber and iron waited on wagons to be loaded onto the ship. Runi took my hand. "Come, Lara. I will take you to a tavern."

"What is a tavern?" I asked.

"You will see. Good food and drinks to celebrate our arrival." Runi's eyes shown brighter than ever and his smile broadened.

We made our way through the crowds. There were more people here than at the Althing in Iceland. I had not experienced a big city before. The sights, sounds, and smells were overpowering. In the midst of the row of colorful structures lining the wharf, Runi led me to a red building with a yellow door. Inside were tables and benches filled with folks noisily eating and talking. Agnas would say it was too early in the day for drinking spirits, but Runi did not seem to remember that. He set our packs down by an empty table and held a chair for me. Once seated, he held up his hand and a maid with a towel folded over her arm approached. Runi said, "Two ales and two beef and breads."

The maid nodded and disappeared behind a door. Runi swept his hand around and beamed at me, "This is a tavern. And you are my wife. And I am a happy man."

I reached over and covered his hand with mine. "And I am happy, too, Husband."

The ale and food arrived and I am quite sure I never enjoyed a meal so much before or ever again. The beef was tender and savory. I would be spoiled for mutton after eating that meal. I savored each sip and bite while taking in the sights and sounds of the lively place. I heard snatches of conversations in languages I did not know and Runi told me that people from Denmark, Germany, the Netherlands, Russia, and England gathered here. He said there might be others as well, but that is all he knew about. "Because the Faroe Islands have so few people, I may be the only Faroese here," he explained. "But because the Norwegian language is so close to the Faroe language, we should not have any trouble talking to people here."

I nodded and smiled, "Ja, and I know some Norwegian from Modir and Fadir. Icelandic is close to Norwegian as well. That is probably why we have been able to understand each other all along."

Runi nodded, then rubbed his forehead and said, "I would like to stay here in Bergen for one night before we begin our journey to Skien to find your people. I know a rooming house where we can rest." He set some coins on the table and we rose to leave. We gathered our packs and walked to the end of the row of colorful buildings. Runi stopped at a blue house with white trim and a flower box out front. "Here," Runi said. He opened the door and a bell tinkled overhead.

"I am coming!" A tall woman with gray hair and eyes and a figure that filled out her traditional Norwegian bunad came down the stairs. "Ah! I was just making up a bedroom. You would like to stay?"

"Ja. I have stayed here once before. Now I bring my wife, Lara."

She peered at Runi and then her face brightened. "Of course. You are the sailor Runi who helped me move furniture last year." She looked at me then, "And welcome to your pretty wife. He is a good worker, your husband. I gave him the room for half-fee because he helped me." She looked at Runi again. "Perhaps you would like a half-fee room in exchange for some heavy lifting again?"

"I will gladly help you. But may we bathe and rest a bit first?"

"Certainly. I will make a list of things I need done while you settle in. Take the first room at the top of the stairs. It is the best room and I just cleaned it." She handed Runi the key with a wink. "Go ahead now, you two."

We went up the stairs slowly. Both of us were sluggish, probably because we indulged so heartily in the ale and food. A pitcher and basin held fresh water. We washed up and fell into the soft, clean bed. I reached for Runi. He took my hand and said, "I hope you will forgive me if I sleep a while. I am exhausted." I looked at his face. How pale and drawn he looked. He seemed fine at the tavern, but I reminded myself that I did wake him out of a sound sleep when we approached the harbor.

"Of course. I am tired, too." I had not slept at all the night before and exhaustion hit me as well. It seemed strange to sleep in the daytime, but I did not awaken until the sky began to dim. Runi was still sound asleep. I sat up and looked at him. He had some flat red spots on his face. I wondered if an insect had bitten him. I put my hand on his forehead and his eyes flew open in alarm.

"What is it?" he asked.

"Nothing," I replied. "You just have some bites on your face. And your forehead feels warm."

He raised himself up on his elbow. "My back aches. Too much pulling on ropes, I guess," he said.

"I will see if anything on the matron's chores are something I can help with. You stay here and rest."

Runi sunk back down onto the bed without a word. I quickly dressed in clean clothes and before I reached the door, he was sleeping again.

CHAPTER 54

The matron turned when she heard me coming down the steps. "What? No Runi?" she asked.

"Nei. He is so tired. I think he wore himself out in the last few weeks preparing for our journey. But I am willing to work if I can help you."

She consulted the list on her slate. "Let me see. The draperies need a good shaking. I can also use some help moving furniture away from walls to clean under and behind. Are you strong and a good cleaner?"

"I can do most things that a man can do." I showed her the muscles in my arms and she chuckled.

"Ja. I see. Let us get started then. We will let Mr. Sleepy be."

We spent the rest of the evening doing chores together, falling into an easy rhythm. After a couple of hours, she suddenly said, "Uff da. I did not tell you my name. How rude of me. I am Anna."

"I do not think you are rude … Anna." I replied.

She smiled and gave a quick nod of approval. Then she said, "What do you think about that husband of yours? Should we offer him some supper? I am hungry and I would guess that you are, too."

"I am hungry," I replied. "I am surprised that Runi has not yet joined us; I will go and see him."

Runi was still sleeping soundly when I went to check on him. His forehead was hot and he did not wake at my touch. I dampened a cloth and placed it on his head. He still did not stir. Hoping to cool his body, I peeled back the blanket that covered him. That is when I saw that spots were on his arms and legs. Alarm bells went off in my head. I remembered stories of the plague that killed many people in the fourteenth century. Fadir told of a ghost ship that was carrying wool from England. Everyone on board died of plague at sea. The corpse ship drifted into Bergen harbor. And now here we were, also in Bergen. I tried to remember what the symptoms of plague or Black Death were. There was something about swelling in the neck and groin, and fingers and toes turning black. I examined Runi for swellings and found none. His fingers and toes were not black, but red spots were developing on his hands and feet. I had to think quickly. I could not tell Anna of his illness. She might not allow us to stay. I would invent a story and conceal his condition so that he could rest and recover here. Ja. That is what I must do.

I lightly covered Runi and joined Anna downstairs in the kitchen. I told her that Runi asked for broth. "We ate a big meal at the tavern when we arrived earlier today and he has done nothing to work up an appetite," I explained.

Anna obliged and I brought a bowl upstairs to Runi. With some effort, I was able to wake him. He was so weak that I had to spoon feed him, holding his head with my free hand. "I am sorry to be a bother," he said. "I should be helping and all I do is sleep."

"You have a strong and capable wife, Runi," I said lightly. "You must rest and tomorrow you will make it up to me." I fervently hoped that he would be better in the morning. I replaced the cloth on his head with a fresh one and arranged the blanket covering him. He again slept, his breathing heavy. I lightly kissed his forehead and closed the door when I left.

When I returned the empty bowl to Anna, she had supper ready for the two of us. We sat and ate a fine fish stew with potatoes and fresh bread. She even had lingonberries to share. What a treat. I told Anna of our planned trip to Skien to find my family. I showed her my silver pendant and told her about my modir's brodir, Tollaf Henriksen, the jeweler.

"That is beautiful," Anna said, "A family treasure."

I nodded and swallowed a bite of bread before I continued. "My little brodir, Ole, has one like it." Mentioning Ole made me suddenly homesick for Modir, Fadir and Ole, but I kept up my falsely cheerful chatter, "The last my fadir knew of his family, they were smelting bog iron and working metals in Skien." Anna listened intently and when I stopped to take another bite, she asked, "So, how is Runi feeling?"

"He will be fine by morning." I tried to sound breezy and unconcerned.

Anna looked at my face. "You are worried."

I laughed but even I could hear that it did not ring true.

Anna closed her eyes for a moment, and then she said, "I like your Runi and I like you, too. If he is ill, you need to tell me. I know some things about healing. Maybe I can help."

I had not considered that Anna might be able to help. I only thought to protect Runi by allowing him a safe place to rest and recover. Dear Jesus, let him recover. Once again, I was in a predicament about confiding in someone. Anna seemed like a kind and generous person, but would she risk exposing herself and other guests to Runi's illness? She watched my face. Then she said, "Do you want me to see him? Or do you want to tell me? Is it more than just weariness?" She laid her hand on my arm and looked at me with pity.

Worry overcame my resistance and I burst into tears. I blurted, "He is suddenly so ill. He is feverish and covered in red spots."

"Quickly," Anna said. "We will fill a tub and to try to bring his fever down."

I helped her carry the large metal tub up the steps and then we carried buckets of water to fill it. "We will add some heated water, too," she said. "We do not want to shock his system." When I emptied the hot water into the tub, the edge burned my arm. I noticed the red welt, but did nothing about it; we had more pressing matters to attend to.

When the tub was sufficiently filled, I was suddenly embarrassed. "I do not think I can lift him by myself."

"Certainly not. I will help you," she replied.

"But he… he is naked."

I could see that Anna was trying not to laugh. "My dear, I have buried two husbands. I know what a naked man looks like. Now let us not delay." She whipped back the blanket. "Into the tub, young man," she said.

Runi roused himself enough to get on his feet. Anna and I took his arms and eased him into the water. With towels, we ran water over his head and shoulders while his chin rested on his chest. Anna felt his neck. "He is still feverish. I will make some medicine for him. Continue to bathe him and I will be right back." Anna bustled out of the room and closed the door.

"Runi," I said. "I am sorry I exposed you to another woman, but I am worried about you." I lifted his face. He did not open his eyes, but he smiled a bit. "She is getting medicine for you." I tenderly kissed him.

Anna burst back into the room. "Here is a tea infused with herbs to help with the fever." She held it to Runi's lips and he tried valiantly to drink. "Lara. Get a spoon." I ran down to the kitchen. When I returned

I smelled the vomit before I saw it. "Help me get him back into the bed. I will clean things up and try the tea again."

We got Runi on his feet and wrestled his large frame back into the bed. I toweled him off some before Anna told me to stop. "He will be cooler if he is damp." I was horrified to see that the spots were becoming pustules and I had opened some to bleeding with the towel. Anna looked up from cleaning the floor. "Lara," she said gently, "Come into the hall with me." She gathered the dirty towels and handed them to me. I slowly left Runi's side and joined her in the hallway. Anna quietly closed the bedroom door. "Lara," she had a look of resolve and sincerity, "Runi has the pox. I have seen it before. My first husband died of smallpox. If Runi lives, he will be disfigured." I just knew that his symptoms meant something terrible. What would I do? I felt like I might fall on the floor. Anna said, "I believe that I am immune because I have been exposed to smallpox before. Look here." She rolled up her left sleeve. "These are scars from pox. I recovered from a mild case. So I can safely nurse your Runi." She smiled at me and then drew me to her. I was stiff and numb. Runi and I had been so happy. Was it only this morning that we shouted "Skol" with the revelers in the tavern? How can my strong dependable husband be so deathly ill? Had I killed him with my desire to come to Norway?

Anna gestured to the room across the hall. "You will sleep here tonight. Although you have no doubt already been exposed, we cannot risk any more that you will become ill, too. Especially in your condition."

I looked at her, confused. "My condition?"

"I know the look of a maid with child. A certain fullness, a glow. We do not want to lose the baby." I marveled that this woman, who I had only met that day, could not only offer to nurse my husband, but also look deep into my soul and see my secrets. I wondered what else she might know about me. Just then we heard Runi groan and I turned to go to him, but

Anna held me back. "The child," she said simply. She opened the bedroom door and I saw Runi lying unmoving on the bed. Anna went in and closed the door. I stood in the darkened hallway, my arms full of soiled towels, staring blankly at the door.

⟨HAPTER 55

I found myself in endless cycles of boiling water, washing towels and blankets, making bone broth, cleaning, and worrying. Although the bed Anna gave me was good, I could not sleep. I was no longer accustomed to sleeping alone and I was cold then hot all night. The lack of sleep and the worry made me irritable and weepy. But I helped as much as I could. I did not want Anna to lose her livelihood because of Runi and me. Already, Anna put a "Closed" sign on the door and locked it, so that no other customers would enter the house. Tending to Runi's every need, Anna diligently ascended and descended the stairs like the biblical angels that Jacob saw on a ladder to heaven in his dream. When not nursing Runi, Anna left briefly each day to retrieve the post, buy fresh food from the wharf market, and catch up on the news.

One day while she was away, I went in to see Runi. Afterwards, I wished I had not. I wished only to think of him as the strong, handsome man I married. As soon as I opened the door, I was hit by the stench of decaying flesh. My eyes burned when I saw him. I was horrified by his appearance. Pustules covered his face. Even his eyelids and ears were disfigured by the hideous bumps. I must have made a sound, because I saw his eyes flutter, but they did not open and I am ashamed to say, I fled the room in a rush and closed the door. I went downstairs and let out the loud sobs that had collected in my throat. Then I leaned over the kitchen basin and vomited until I felt all my insides had been purged. I sunk down onto a chair in the kitchen and buried my head in my arms. I railed against God. "How can you allow him to be ravaged so? What has Runi ever done but be good and true? He does not deserve this." And then my tone changed to one of supplication. "Please do not let him suffer. Please do not let him die." and then, "Tell him I love him. Tell him I will take care of our baby. Tell him…."

I heard Anna's key in the lock and then the shutting and locking of the door. I quickly wiped my face with my apron. Anna came into the kitchen and set packages down, then sat herself down. Hard. She slowly shook her head from side to side. "What is it, Anna?" I asked.

"The pox. Runi is not the only one. The epidemic is spreading like a forest fire through the entire continent. They say the merchant ships are bringing infected folks into ports, like Bergen. Of course, I did not say anything about Runi. But there were questions about why my boarding house is closed. I said that I have a young couple helping me with some deep cleaning. But this cannot go on too much longer. If it is discovered that we have the pox in my house, we will be quarantined."

I tried to sort through my options. But there were really no good options until we knew if Runi would live. I took a deep breath. "Anna," I looked into her somber gray eyes. "Will Runi die?"

Anna's eyes searched mine before she answered. "Only God knows for certain, but I do not think he can go on much longer. His breathing is now labored; he no doubt has the swellings in his throat. I doubt he will live through another night."

I looked down at my belly and slowly nodded. After seeing him, I think I knew he could not survive. When I finally looked up, Anna was studying me. "Your neck and face are blotchy." She glanced at the basin.

"And you vomited." Anna put her cool hand on the back of my neck. "You feel a bit warm, but not feverish. Maybe you should go and lie down."

"I will do that. Just for a bit." I trudged from the kitchen and got to the bottom step before I collapsed. When I awoke on a makeshift bed on the reception room floor, I was wearing a clean shift and a bandage wrapped around my head. I winced when I felt a large lump above my right ear. Anna came downstairs and I slowly sat up. The room spun. "What has happened?" I asked.

Anna knelt on the floor by me and drew me into a firm embrace. She began to rock from side to side and then she began a low keening that increased in volume and pitch. I melted into Anna's bosom and allowed myself to rock and keen with her. I continued long after Anna had fallen silent, but she did not let go. She held me that way until I was spent. Later, in soft and comforting tones she told me what I already knew: that Runi had died. And, after falling on the steps, I lost the baby.

CHAPTER 56

Responding to a summons from Anna, strong men -- covered from head to toe -- arrived and took charge. A communal pyre was formed on a stony outcropping of the harbor and there, what remained of Runi and much of the contents of the room where he died, were burned. The sickening sweet stench of burning flesh and the unmistakable acrid odor of burning hair hung in smoky clouds over the town for weeks. Anna and I cleaned and re-cleaned every corner of her house. We did not hurry. We both moved as if in a dream, slowly and without talking. Work was a comfort. I plunged my hands into the hottest water possible and felt it as relief. I scrubbed every surface until I felt my shoulders would break from my body. Almost overnight, my dark shiny hair became dry and brittle, and a white streak appeared, covering the place where I hit my head. My clothes hung like wet laundry on my diminishing frame. I did not want to be alive.

After a time, it felt as though I had always lived in that dream state at Anna's house. I could hardly remember living in Iceland or the Faroe Islands. It all seemed like a story from someone else's life. Anna did not try to wake me from my dream state. She gently went about her business and fed and clothed me as if I were a small child who could not fend for herself. I continued to clean whatever I saw. Any dirt or filth was vanquished with grim vigor. Summer came and went and cool, fresh breezes began to fill the house. The threat of smallpox had abated. Just as quickly as it swept through communities, leaving families bereft, it was gone.

After supper one evening, Anna drew a letter from her pocket and slid it across the table to me. I picked it up and turned it over and over, examining it as if it were a magic trick. A fine spidery script spelled out my name on heavy paper that was folded and sealed with wax. Hot tears filled my eyes until I could no longer see. I felt like I had lost everything, but someone was reaching out to me. My name was there in ink. Except for the note that Modir had given me when I left for Thingvellir, I had never received a letter. I gently set it back down onto the table. The tears spilled out onto my lap.

Anna spoke in a quiet voice, as if we were in church. "Lara, I wrote to your modir's brodir Tollef in Skien. I believe he has written this letter to you." She pushed it closer to me. "Open it."

I picked it up again and slid my finger under the seal. It popped open to reveal a whole page of the lovely handwriting:

Dearest Lara,

How we have longed to know how my dottir and her family have fared since leaving for Iceland all those years ago. And now you are grown and here in Norway. Your bestemor and I would like to fetch you to come and live with us for as long as it suits you. We are healthy and have a comfortable life and would be honored to share what we have with you. At the start of the new moon, we plan to arrive in Bergen by ship. If you would be so kind as to accept our offer, we would like to bring you back to Skien with us. Even if you decide not to accompany us back home, we want to see you.

Your loving bestefar,
Christopher Henriksen

My grandparents. I did not know they lived. My mouth hung open and I dropped the letter on the table. The wish to go to Skien had been lost in my grief, but the letter brought a spark of desire back to me. I blinked and looked around the room as if I had not seen it before. Anna caught my eye and smiled. My eyes filled again, but this time when tears fell, it was because I smiled.

CHAPTER 57

"Do you think that you will go?" Anna asked. "If you want to stay, there is a home for you here."

How simple it would be to stay here with Anna until I could return to my family in Iceland. But this house held the memory of a terrible time. And Runi brought me here to Norway to find my family. I should honor him by doing that. I studied Anna's kind face that had become so familiar to me. "I am forever grateful to you, Anna. I am sorely tempted to stay with you, but I feel I should go. I have not asked or even really been curious before now, but would you please tell me why you have been so kind to Runi -- and to me?"

"Over the past months that you have been with me, I have pondered this." She folded and re-folded the letter as she talked. "Before you arrived, I had been feeling lonely, keeping the boarding house by myself since my second husband died a little over two years ago." Anna looked out the window. "I feel foolish telling you about the next part."

I waited while Anna appeared to be gathering her thoughts, or maybe the courage to reveal them.

Finally she continued, "I hope you will not think me daft or absurd. I had a dream shortly before you and Runi arrived. A short woman with a furry face came to me in the dream." She looked at me then. "It is foolish," she said.

"Nei," I replied, "I know her. It is Hildur. She is Huldufolk. She has helped me before."

Anna looked at me as if I had grown a carrot for a nose. "She has a name? And you know her?"

"Ja. Did Hildur speak to you in your dream?"

"She told me someone needed my help and I would know what to do. Shortly after you two arrived, I began to believe that the dream – your Hildur – came so that I would help you and Runi." She shrugged and smiled, "So I did. And... you helped me, too. I am no longer lonely."

"If I go to Skien, will you be all right?" I asked.

"Of course, dear Lara. I will be fine." She patted my hand, then turned it over and placed the letter in my palm. "This is why Runi brought you here. If you are inclined, I think you should go. You can come back to stay with me anytime." She pushed up my sleeve. "Good. The pockmarks that formed where the burn was are completely healed. I think I know how you got the marks. No doubt the infected towels you carried rubbed on it. Some folks do that intentionally, thinking it wards off the disease. They scrape a coin across a pustule of an infected person and introduce the pus into a cut in their healthy skin. Thank God, you did not get the pox. The scars on your arm protect you, just as my pock mark protects me." She pushed up her sleeve and held her scarred arm by mine.

I nodded. We had been through so much. What would I do without Anna's kindness? I was unsteady and unsure. But even in my uncertainty, I resolved that I would go to Skien. And then I would go home to Iceland.

CHAPTER 58

During the days just before the arrival of the new moon, I went outside often to see the ships newly docked. I did not want to miss the arrival of my grandparents. Finally, as promised, the new moon brought the ship from Skien to Bergen. An older couple, stately and sturdy, made their way down the wharf. I knew them at once. Their features and bearing were like Modir's. They knew me, too. With his traveling case in one hand, Bestefar raised his other to Anna and me, then rushed over to throw his arm around me. "Lara!" he exclaimed. Bestemor, dressed in a beautiful well-worn bunad held me in a long embrace.

I had bathed and plaited my hair, the white streak impossible to hide. The shift I last wore at my wedding hung in deep folds. The paleness of my face showed that I had remained indoors during the months of mourning. For a maid who just passed seventeen years, I felt that I looked like an old matron. Nevertheless, I could not stop smiling. Agnas and Anna had been unfailingly kind to me, but these were my people. I wanted to know everything about them.

After exchanging introductions and news of their voyage, Anna welcomed them to the boarding house and showed them a room, thankfully, not the one Runi died in with its bad memories. We had prepared a special meal and once Bestemor and Bestefar had settled in, they joined us in the dining room. I had to giggle. We could not stop staring at each other. "You look so much like your modir when she left for Iceland," Bestemor said.

"And you both resemble her as well," I said. "I wish I had, but I never asked why Modir and Fadir left Norway. Do you know?"

Bestefar and Bestemor exchanged glances. "You tell," Bestemor said.

Bestefar set his spoon down and looked at me with his soft gray eyes. "Your fadir did not take to working the metal as his family does. He wanted to be a farmer. Land is scarce for farming here. Too many mountains. When they married, they decided to try for Iceland."

Bestemor said, "We were sad to see them go, but we tried to understand. Bestefar loves the land, too. He wishes we had been so brave as young folks." She turned to Bestefar, "Is that not true?"

Bestefar nodded, "Ja, but leaving family is hard. Tollef, who Anna's letter was addressed to, moved to Trondheim, near the Nideros Cathedral. He sent by post a drawing he made of the cathedral. It is large and very beautiful." Bestefar looked wistfully over my head, then back at me. "Someday maybe we will go there to see him. He has a thriving jewelry business. Pilgrims and holy men covet his work."

I pulled the pendant from under my shift. "Modir gave me this. He made it."

Bestemor peered at the silver. "That is his signature piece. She pulled a chain from her bodice. "See? Here is mine." The pendant and chain were similar to the one I wore.

"Modir said in a note that Ole has one, too." I said.

"Ole?" Bestemor and Bestefar exchanged glances.

"Ja. My little brodir. He would be… four years old now."

"Ah! Are there more children in your family, too?" Bestemor asked.

"Nei. Just Ole and me. Since I received the letter from you, I wondered that Modir never wrote to you."

"Sending post is expensive. And your mor and far may have thought that we did not wish to hear from them." Bestefar explained. "We were not glad about their choice to move away. When they left, we did not give them our blessing. We regret that we had no way to contact them afterward or to know of you and Ole." He sighed deeply and then smiled broadly, "But now we have you, and the broken circle is mended."

"And my fadir's family?"

Bestefar's face fell. "Most of your far's family died of pox last year. It swept through their household. Only one of your fetters remains."

I had not considered that my fadir's brodirs and systirs would have children my age. "I would like to meet him." I said.

"Ja. You will meet everyone. But your fetter is not a lad, but an unmarried maid about your age. Dorthe."

"Dorthe," I repeated. I did not know why, but I felt that I liked her already.

Bestemor and Bestefar explained that the ship would be leaving for Skien the next morning. I would need to pack my things and bid farewell to Anna before dawn. I looked at Anna. She smiled, but her eyes were full. I wished I could both stay and go. But after the long, painful months of mourning for Runi and our baby, I was finally sensing some eagerness in my spirit. I had to go.

CHAPTER 59

I tossed and barely slept that night, my mind in a swirl. Finally hearing waking voices, I was relieved to get up and start the day. I changed my bedding and straightened my room, readying it for Anna's next guests. I smoothed the blanket one final time, feeling a bit melancholy to leave this place, but then the clatter of pots downstairs called me to breakfast. I took my pack and closed the door. In the kitchen, Anna was putting soft sweet bread on a plate. "I will carry the food to the dining room," I said.

There, Bestemor and Bestefar were already enjoying Anna's coffee, newly arrived on a ship from the Caribbean. "Good morning, Lara," Bestemor said. "Do you like coffee?"

"I have only tasted it twice before," I said, "Anna said some folks like it with milk and even some sugar. I have tried it that way, but I think I like it best plain. It is supposed to give you energy."

"I had better have more, then," Bestefar said, "I was eager for our trip and did not sleep much. Lara, I was thinking about our talk yesterday. When family members move away, ja. It is hard. But it is also generous. It leaves more for those who are left at home. Our family's wealth has grown. And I hope your far got land in Iceland."

"We are crofters on the Arnesen farm. Fadir does not complain, but I am sure he would like his own land."

"Maybe someday, eh?" Bestefar said.

When Anna joined us, Bestemor said, "Anna, we have brought you gifts in gratitude for taking care of our Lara." She gave a package to Anna. "Please open it."

Anna looked from them to me, and said, "It was my pleasure. And Lara worked very hard. I will miss her." She carefully untied the bundle and held up an apron with colorfully embroidered flowers at the waist and bottom. "It is beautiful. Did you do the handwork?"

Bestemor nodded, "There is another small package as well."

Anna unwrapped a silver brooch of ancient design. When she held it up, the light of dawn coming through the window caught the dangling silver disks and they sparkled. She put her hand on her chest, "Merciful Jesus," she said, "I have never owned something so lovely."

"Wear it in good health and with our best regards," Bestefar said. "Our dottir's mann, Knud, made it. If you are ever in need of funds, you can sell it."

"I will cherish it always," Anna stood and put on the apron, then pinned the brooch to her bodice. She slowly turned in a circle. "I feel like a young bride." We all laughed.

"But now, the time has come that we must leave you," Bestefar said.

I tearfully bid Anna farewell, and with a final firm embrace, I joined Bestemor and Bestefar on the wharf. There, the ship that would take us to Skien waited. When we reached the top deck, I looked back at Anna and waved. A chapter of my tale closed, but another began.

CHAPTER 60
BERGEN TO PORSGRUNN TO SKIEN NORWAY

This voyage, sharing a cabin with my grandparents, was much different from the one Runi and I took from the Faroe Islands less than a year earlier. This was a Norwegian vessel that served its coastal communities as transportation, postal service, and delivery vehicle. The ship was clean and efficient, and as a bonus, it stopped for a few hours at a number of ports along the route, so I had an opportunity to disembark and explore.

The first port we stopped at was Haugesund. There we saw the remnants of an ancient Viking village with many buildings still standing along the shores of the misty bay. One of the buildings was occupied and when we strolled past, a man greeted us and told stories of the village. He showed us the round pagan chapel with a figurehead of Odin on its roof, drying sheds like the ones we used on the Faroe Islands, and he pointed out the drowning rock, a place where criminals were tied up to face the rising tide. I thought about the Althings and of all the creative ways folks invented to eliminate the wrong-doers among them. Although the weather was not cold, I shivered. I could have easily been a victim of harsh punishment, myself.

Next we visited Stavanger where we walked cobbled streets and admired colorful wooden houses built on rock. Bestemor reminded me of the parable in the Bible that said we should build on rock, not sand.

"The story is about making God the basis for your life, of course," Bestemor said, "But I would venture to say that these houses will stand a long time." From time to time on the journey, I would catch Bestemor or Bestefar studying me. They no doubt were curious about my great sadness, but they did not pry.

Christianssand was the next port. We saw the large stone fortress that was built on orders of King Christian IV over fifty years earlier. "Since Christianssand is the southernmost port in Norway," Bestefar explained, "It is a strategic place from which to defend the country from invaders."

That evening, while we ate our supper on the ship, Bestefar said, "Tomorrow night we will be in Porsgrunn, the port nearest Skien. That is where we will disembark." After supper, we bundled up and went on deck where we saw a fantastic display of the Aurora. I thought about seeing the swirling, magical colors with Runa and Runi and my chest ached with missing them, and Agnas and Raven, too. I promised myself once again that I would visit my Faroese family and tell them the sad news of Runi's death.

In the morning, when the ship approached Porsgrunn, Bestemor said, "Gather your things and we will go on deck." From there, I could see the port's harbor lined with buildings that were not as colorful as in some of the other cities we visited. This was a working town of trade, fisheries, and iron. We approached the wharf and Bestemor raised her handkerchief and began waving. A gathered group also began to wave and shout. "Look, Lara, your family has come to meet you and bring us home."

We were greeted by beaming faces as we disembarked. I could not have imagined such a welcome. "Ah, she looks like her mor," and "I am your mor's soster." "Let me look at you." "You look hungry. Are you hungry? We have food at the house." I was overwhelmed by all the vaguely familiar, comfortable faces of my kin. I smiled and nodded, and soon I was hustled, along with Bestemor and Bestefar, onto a small wagon with our packs. Another larger wagon quickly filled with family members and followed us along a path that ran parallel the water. I was astounded by the bounty of wood used for buildings, walkways, horse paths, boats, crates, barrels, and still there were dense forests all around. We passed some logs floating down the waterway toward the harbor and boats low in the water, carrying iron ore. Family members waved to the boats as they passed. Soon we arrived at the homestead, a cluster of buildings that housed all the family. Bestefar stopped his horse by a log home with glass windows and a slate roof. It was as fine – or maybe finer – than Anna's Bergen house. We entered a cozy hearth room. Bestemor said, "Come, Lara, I will show you your room." She led me to a sturdy door with an iron latch that opened to a tidy bed, a table and lamp, and a woolen rug on the floor. I set my pack down and looked at Bestemor's happy face. I sat on the bed and smoothed the soft blanket under me.

"Was this my modir's … my mor's room?" I asked.

"When your mor was here, we had only a small log hut with a sod roof. The extra rooms have been added over the years."

"I know of Tollef, mor's bror and I just met her soster. Does she have other bror and soster?"

"You met your fraenka Sara, her soster. She and her family live here on the homestead, in the house on the other side of the stabbur." I wondered what a stabbur was. Bestemor's face grew solemn. "My sonn, Hans, drowned when he was only twenty years old." Her face brightened once again. "If you are ready, we will go eat with the others. Soon you will put all of the faces and names together."

Outside, we passed a wooden shed that was larger on the top than on the bottom. "What is this used for?" I asked.

"Ah. The stabbur is a storage shed for food. Do you not have them in Iceland?"

"Nei. Not like this. Why is it on stilts?"

"To keep pests out. See? The steps do not join the building for the same reason. The hay has been drying on the fence for a few weeks. Soon we will bring it into the stabbur to feed the sheep and horses over the winter. Now that cold weather has arrived, the cheeses, butter, and meats that have been cooling in the mountain springs will be brought into the stabbur for winter storage." Bestemor climbed the steps and produced a key from her belt. "Here. We will look inside." The building was mostly empty. "We will sweep it clean before re-filling it." She closed the door again and locked it. She held out her belt. "My wife keys. Is that a custom in Iceland as well?"

"Ja." I was sad that my woven belt never held wife keys. Runi did not live to make a homestead of our own. I wondered if my belt would ever hold keys. I absently rubbed the wedding tattoo on my finger.

When we entered the home of modir's soster, Sara, the comforting, familiar aroma of mutton stew and bread greeted me. Then the rush of people. I met Sara's mann, Onkel Knud, and my fetters Lars, Johannes, and Elisabeth and their little children. They were playing a game of Hide the Thimble while waiting for their meal.

This meal was the first of many I shared with my modir's Norwegian family. We all gathered at Sara and Knud's home for each mid-day meal, pausing from our various chores. I helped Bestemor with household tasks, but also worked outside alongside the others, hauling hay to the stabbur, taking the horse up to the mountain stream to retrieve the dairy goods that cooled there, helping with the sheep, and most exciting – learning metalwork.

I was curious to know about the ironwork, since both Fadir's and Modir's families were all employed in some kind of metalwork, so Lars invited me to visit the Fossom Ironworks where he worked. There, men collected and processed bog mud to produce iron. Even on a cold autumn day, the heat of the fire and metal was fierce; I could not imagine working in the smelter in humid summer heat. Straw fed the fire that removed moisture and impurities from the iron. I watched as the men poured molten iron into molds to form door latches and hinges, locks and keys, anchors, lamps, cooking pots, and grave crosses. Some made parts that would be assembled into stoves and even cannons. The metal work reminded me of weaving: creating something useful and beautiful from raw materials. Flushed and excited, I went to Bestefar with a request, "May I borrow trousers and a tunic from you? I want to work with Fetter Lars and the men at the Ironworks."

Bestefar looked at me with wide eyes, "Will the men want you there?"

"Lars said I could help him, if I wanted to."

Bestefar then had a bemused smile and looked at Bestemor. "What do you think, Bestemor? Would you agree to that?"

She smoothed the tangle of hair from my brow and looked into my eyes. "I see a spark here that should not be extinguished. Fetch the clothes, Bestefar. And your old coat, too." Then she turned to me, "Do you have a hat and mittens?"

"Ja. From Agnas."

Bestefar appeared then with the clothes and held them out to me. "They will be much too big for you. Maybe you can fix them?" I ran to my bedroom and returned with my colorful woven belt.

"I will hold the trousers up with this."

"Tisk. Tisk." said Bestemor. "That is much too lovely for that dirty work. Here." She produced a length of sturdy rope. "Just for now."

"Tusen Takk." I took the clothes to my bedroom and put them on. They were right; Bestefar was not stout, but he was certainly larger and taller than me. I cinched the rope around my waist and rolled up the legs and sleeves. Then I put on my hat and mittens and emerged to show Bestefar and Bestemor. They chuckled and applauded. And I was surprised to realize that I felt happy.

CHAPTER 61

The next morning, Bestemor asked if she could braid my hair for me before Lars arrived to bring me to work. I fetched the bone comb that she had given to Modir and Modir had given to me. Bestemor turned it over in her hands, tenderly looking at it like she was seeing the face of an old friend. "This untangled your mor's hair, too," she said. "Tell me. Has her hair any gray in it? I have not seen her in so long."

"Nei. Her hair is still brown and shiny." Bestemor nodded, then motioned for me to sit. She took my long wavy hair in her hand and patiently worked the comb in sections through the snarls from the ends to my scalp. She touched the place where I had hit my head on the steps at Anna's, and re-combed the white streak in my dark hair. "I wonder how this happened?" she asked. As she continued to comb my hair, I told her about Runi's illness and death, and my miscarriage. I took comfort in her gentle hands, but still, I felt deep heaviness in my spirit.

When she finished braiding and coiling my hair, I stood and she took my face in her hands. "My darling girl," she said. "I know you do not believe it now, but it will get easier as time goes on. You will never get over it, but it will get easier." She took the hat that Agnas knitted for me and stretched it over my thick braids. "There. Now you will stay warm. Warm head, warm body."

The door latch clicked and in walked Lars. He looked at my trousers with surprise, but only said, "Ready to go, Lara?"

I was ready.

We arrived at Fossom, and some of the men scoffed at a maid learning ironwork. "She should learn bread work," one of the men said. The others laughed and another added, "Ja. Or needle work." I wanted to tell them that I already knew how to cook and sew, but I did not want to argue. I wanted to learn. A few of the men remarked about my clothing. "Fyfaen! A maid should wear maid's clothing." "What kind of maid wears lads' trousers?" "No man wants to see that."

Lars kept me close by his side. "I will help you as much as I can," Lars said, "But I have to keep up with my own work, too. Watch what I do. Then we will gather some scraps that you can use to forge your own piece." I could see that this was indeed hard work. Even in the cold weather, the men were in shirtsleeves. The odors of the smoky fire, the acrid molten metal, and the sweaty, smelly men made me glad that we were outdoors. I stepped away from time to time for a big breath of fresh air. I made myself useful by working the bellows until my arm ached. Lars lifted the heavy cauldron of molten metal with thick mittens to pour it into sand molds. Seeing that I was in earnest, the other men began to soften their attitudes toward me. Slowly, a pile of metal scraps that I could experiment with grew larger as the men casually dropped scraps as they passed by. After making some buttons and nails, I created a grave cross for Runi. Lars showed me how to alter the mold to include Runi's name and the date of his death. I made a small sand mold and poured another cross for our baby. None of the iron claimed from the bog was wasted. I helped to load fingers of ore onto a wagon to be delivered to a blacksmith in the village. When finally the castings had cooled, I knocked the crosses from the molds, and I was glad to see that they were acceptable.

That Sunday, we took the crosses with us to the Gjerpen Kirke. I insisted on carrying them myself from the wagon to the graveyard, their weight like a needed tether, keeping me from blowing away. I wished that Runi were with me now. He was always so strong and brave. Bestefar gently took the crosses from me and pounded them into the hard ground near the other family gravestones and crosses. The preacher joined us and said a prayer. A sob caught in my throat and Bestemor held me close so that my cries were muffled in the warmth of her embrace. Bestefar cleared his throat and shuffled his feet. I wiped my face with my mitten. Bestemor said, "Let us go home now." She took my hand and led me to the wagon.

Onkle Knud approached me after Sunday meal. "Lars tells me you took to the metalwork. Would you like to see what a jeweler does? I am not as talented as Tollaf, but you are welcome to visit my workshop."

"I would very much like to learn jewelry making," I said.

"Tomorrow then," he rubbed his chin. "I hear that you sometimes wear men's clothing. This is clean work for the most part. I will give you a sturdy apron to wear." I wondered how much my relatives talked about me. The men's clothing was no doubt an embarrassment, or at least bafflement to them. If not for Runa, I would never have thought to wear men's clothing, but I liked the freedom it afforded me. Climbing and riding were certainly simpler. For many tasks, the trousers were more practical. The only thing that was easier about women's skirts was using the outhouse.

The next day I arrived at Knud's shop wearing a skirt with a men's tunic. A compromise. He gave me a heavy sailcloth apron to wear and I sat on a stool next to him at his workbench. First he showed me how to pound the silver thin into a smooth, even wire. I spent a lot of time perfecting that skill. Then he showed me how to braid the wire as the Vikings did to create a fine chain. My first attempts were uneven, but soon I was able to make a smooth rope of chain. Then I learned the same techniques, only using copper, which felt a bit different than the silver. One day, I brought Tryggve's carved knife to show him. He turned it over and over in his hands, admiring the craftsmanship. "Your Icelandic friend has some great talent," he said.

Over time, he taught me to make simple shawl pins, hook earrings, and rings for different sizes of fingers. When I finished a wide silver ring with some twining engraving, I slipped it on my finger to admire it. It completely covered my wedding tattoo. Someday, I thought, I may be ready to cover it, but not today. Onkel Knud glanced over at me, "That is some fine work. You are right to admire it."

I quickly removed the ring, "I hope you do not think me impertinent. I am not hoping to keep it."

"I did not think you were," Knud resumed his work. "I will take whatever is not sold in Skien to Porsgrunn. The pieces you have made will fetch a good price."

I was proud to think that my work would help to support the family. And I liked learning new skills. But something nagged at me. "Onkel Knud, do you think I could visit Dorthe, my fetter from my fadir's family? I understand she is alone since the pox took her family."

Knud wiped and arranged his tools on a rack. "Talk to your Bestefar and Bestemor. I am quite sure that can be arranged. She lives in Bo, about a half-day's ride from here."

CHAPTER 62

That evening after supper, Bestefar sat by the hearth smoking his pipe, silently reading his Bible. Bestemor was mending some stockings. I brought out my drop-spindle and some wool to spin into yarn and sat by the fire with them. I was a bit afraid to bring up my desire to visit Dorthe. I did not know if they would be offended that I wanted to leave their home, even for a short time. Finally, I summoned the courage to speak. "Do you think I could go and visit Dorthe in Bo sometime before winter weather hinders travel?"

Neither grandparent responded. I wondered if I should repeat myself. Then Bestefar cleared his throat and closed his Bible. He looked at Bestemor who did not look up. Then he looked at me. "It is late in the season to travel. You may be able to get there, but depending on how long you stay, you may not be able to return when you want to. Winter comes swift and hard."

Bestemor nodded and continued to sew. "We would worry about you," she said.

I did not answer. Bestefar got up, opened the door, and pounded out his pipe on the siding. Then he slowly closed the door, sat again, and stared at the fire. After a long silence he said, "I could take you with the small wagon and fetch you again."

Bestemor's head snapped up. She gave him a stern look and faintly shook her head. "She may miss yuletide with the family if she goes now," she said.

Bestefar displayed a sudden temper, "You indulge her in wearing men's clothing and working alongside the men, but when I want to let her travel, you object."

Bestemor sighed, "You are right, dear Bestefar. If you want to take her and bring her back, I will not object – again," she added.

Bestefar harrumphed, "That is all right then. Lara, when do you want to go? I would say the sooner the better."

The whole exchange between them set me off kilter. I did not remember Modir and Fadir having a disagreement in my presence. I was glad it was settled, but I did not like being the cause of discord between them.

"If you are sure it is agreeable," I looked at Bestemor. She shrugged and tilted her head toward Bestefar as if to say 'Talk to him.' I looked at Bestefar then. "Tomorrow?"

"Fine," he said. "First thing tomorrow I will get Brownie and the wagon ready. You might ready your pack tonight so we can leave as soon as light breaks."

"Ja. I will do that." I collected my spinning and bent to give Bestemor a kiss on my way to my bedroom.

She reached out and hugged me tightly.

"I will come back, Bestemor. I promise."

Bestefar said, "Tomorrow then. Wife: to bed." I ducked into my bedroom. My grandparents could work out their differences without me as a witness. Uff da!

CHAPTER 63
BO NORWAY

When Bestefar knocked on my bedroom door, I thought it was still nighttime; I slept deeply and dreamed of Runi. In my dream, we were at home with Agnas and Runa, sleeping together in our cozy badsofa. I reluctantly sat up and rubbed my face. Then I saw my pack waiting by the bedroom door and remembered that I was traveling today. Quickly, I put on my boots, and grabbed my coat, hat, and mittens. Bestemor had breakfast porridge ready and had even sprinkled some brown sugar on the top. "A little treat for you," she said.

Bestefar finished quickly. "I will wait outside for you." I knew that meant I had better hurry up.

"Lara, you have brought youthful spirit to this house. You remind me of my Hans. He had an interesting and artistic soul." Bestemor sighed. "Come back to us, Lara."

"I will come back, Bestemor. Truly." I kissed her cheek and put on my coat.

"Safe travels," she waved. Bestefar was outside, talking to Brownie and jiggling the reins. They were both impatient to go. The daylight was beginning to cast gray shadows on the ground. I was glad we had not left any earlier; the cloudy sky would have made it pitch black outside.

I climbed onto the wagon and Bestefar covered me with a heavy blanket.

"Ready?" he asked. I was about to answer when Brownie whinnied in reply. We laughed.

When we had traveled a ways, Bestefar said, "Your bestemor has mentioned Hans to you. I want to tell you about him." Bestefar's breath came out in puffy clouds in the cold air. "He was what some call a 'sensitive' lad. He did not like to wrestle or fight. The other lads teased him. He helped me with chores, but preferred to spend his days indoors with Bestemor. He made beautiful wooden carvings and engraved jewelry. Tollaf and Knud learned much of that skill from Hans. I will show you sometime the wooden bowls he painted fanciful flowers and animals on. Bestemor keeps them locked in a cabinet. We will have to ask her for the key."

"I think I would have liked Hans," I said.

"Oh, ja. He was kind and good with children and animals. But he suffered from a lack of friends. More and more toward the end, he spent time alone in the mountains and in the woods." Bestefar took a deep breath and it shuddered when he exhaled. "One spring evening, we could not find him when it was time for supper. He did not come home at all that night. We worried that a wild animal might have attacked him. The next day, we assembled a search group. It was not long before a neighbor whistled. When we got to him, the neighbor had already dragged Hans' body from the spring. We would have thought it was an accident if Hans had not left a note under a rock nearby. Lara," Bestefar's voice broke, "My beautiful lad drowned himself." Bestefar wiped his face on his sleeve. "I am an old fool," he said, "He has been gone longer than he was with us and still I cry like a baby." I patted his arm. "Bestemor blamed herself. She wondered if she could have saved him. We all felt that way. I sometimes think that Tollaf moved to Trondheim to get away from the memory of Hans."

I nodded, "I felt that way about leaving Bergen. Bad memories can linger in a place, I think. Did Hans die after my modir and fadir moved to Iceland?"

"Ja. Your mor does not know that Hans died. He was the youngest child of Bestemor and me. Next was Tollaf. Then your mor. Sara is the oldest. Your modir and Sara shared a room, but not much else. I think Sara was too bossy to your modir." Bestefar chucked. "And Sara is still bossy." He shook his head, "No wonder your Onkle Knud spends so much time in his jewelry shop."

We rode in silence for a bit. I thought about Modir leaving her family for Iceland, and then I began to wonder about how Modir, Fadir, and Ole fared. Had the pox affected the people in Iceland as well? And the Faroe Islands? I wondered how Agnas and Runa were. When I returned to the Faroes, I would have to tell them about Runi and when I got to Iceland after my three years of exile were completed this summer, I would tell Modir about Hans. And Fadir's family all gone. So many families have lost dear ones. I dreaded being the one to bear the bad news. Bestefar looked over at me and I realized I had not responded to his stories.

"Takk for telling me about Hans. That was not easy." I said.

"Hoo. Ja. Not easy," he said. "But telling the story has made the time pass quickly and look. We are nearing Bo. Do you see the big white church on the hill? It is an ancient church. Maybe Dorthe will take you there."

"I would like that. Bestefar, would you be terribly disappointed if I stayed with Dorthe until the spring thaw? I am not sure, of course, but I may be of help to her, since she is the only one of her kin who survived the pox."

"I thought you might be thinking that way. Probably best that you did not bring it up before we left Bestemor. There is fairly regular post between Bo and Skien. Your mor and far courted with letters. Did you know that?" I shook my head. "Ja. It was quite the big romance." He said it like Roooommmance and rolled his eyes. Then he smiled and winked at me. "Anyway, send a letter when you want me to fetch you. I will smooth things over with Bestemor."

We approached a cluster of buildings and Bestefar pointed. "Your fadir's family homestead."

CHAPTER 64

Brownie pulled the wagon onto the path in front of the house. By the time we stopped, Dorthe had come outside, wiping her hands on a towel. Her eyes widened as she recognized Bestefar. "Christopher Henriksen. And a friend. What brings you my way?"

"Dorthe. Nice to see you are well. We were sorry to hear about your family." Bestefar paused and placed his hat over his heart. "But here -- I brought a surprise. This is your fetter, Lara, from Iceland."

Dorthe dropped the towel she was holding and put her hand to her mouth. Her eyes filled. "I have a fetter who lives? What miracle is this?" I jumped from the wagon and she ran to me. I felt an immediate connection to her. We embraced and then she held me away by my shoulders. "Let me see you. Ah, ja. Our family's eyes for sure. And something around the mouth." She studied my face a bit longer and then hugged me again. "Lara!" she exclaimed. Then she said, "Christopher. Come in and get warm. How long can you stay?" She took my arm and led me through the door. Bestefar followed.

He put his hat back on and took it off again and scratched his head, "I can stay for only a while. I want to return home before dark. Lara, however...." He turned to me with his eyebrows raised.

"I will stay, if you will have me," I said. "Perhaps I can be of some help and companionship to you." I thought of Hans' terrible loneliness and was glad of my offer.

"God bless you! Ja! My house is your house."

She made hot tea for us and brought out some bread and brown cheese. Her house was like our house in Iceland with a loft above the main floor. Dorthe was not the best housekeeper. The house was clean but cluttered. I felt confident that I could make sense of her disarray. Bestefar drank his tea and ate some bread and the sweet cheese. Silence followed, then, "It has been a good year for grain, but the sheep are extra wooly; that means a hard winter is coming." He worked his worn fingers around the rim of his hat. "Of course, you know that, Dorthe."

Dorthe nodded and smiled. "Ja. Same here. I was glad to get the hay in the stabbur before heavy snow."

Bestefar nodded and looked out the window. "Ja. Snow can come anytime." He finished his last sip of tea and stood, "I must be on my way." I stood as he put his coat on. "Lara, give me a hug."

His bulky coat and strong arms felt like a big bear embracing me. "Takk, Bestefar."

"Let us hear from you," he said as he went out the door.

Dorthe and I let cold air in the house while we waved goodbye and watched Brownie take Bestefar away. Dorthe then drew me inside and closed the door. "Well!" she said, "You are a most welcome surprise. We have a lot to know about each other, I am sure." She put another log on the fire and gestured for me to sit down. She poured more tea and joined me. "So! You start."

Her warm gaze and easy manner drew the words from me that I had not uttered since leaving home. I told her about life at home with Modir and Fadir and Ole, the Arnesen twins and their reputation, the trip to the Thing in Iceland, about Edda's pregnancy, about Pjetur's death and even my role in it. When I got to that part, she drew in a sharp breath. She sat on the edge of her chair, leaning forward, her eyes fixed on my face. "I hope you do not judge me," I said.

"Nei. I am enthralled by all that you have done. Tell me more."

I continued on, telling of the appearance of Hildur, the raft, the rescue by Runa and Runi, my life in the Faroe Islands, the Althing there, my romance with Runi. Dorthe fanned herself. "Maybe I should not have put that other log on the fire. It is getting warm in here. But please. Go on."

The trip with Runi and all that happened at Anna's house in Bergen tumbled out and when I revealed that he had died of the pox, tears rolled down her cheeks. I told her that I also lost the baby and she said, "Wait. I must get a kerchief." She wiped her face and loudly blew her nose. "But how did you get here?"

The arrival of the letter and then of Bestemor and Bestefar came next, followed by meeting my modir's family and all that I learned during my time in Skien. "And now I am here. That is all," I said.

"All? All? You have lived ten lifetimes and you are only – how old are you?

"I am eighteen years now."

"I am twenty years," she said. "I have never left Bo. My life is completely dull."

"But you have suffered great loss," I said. "And that has no doubt made you wise."

She considered that and then said, "Perhaps you are right. Suffering makes one know what is important."

"Tell me about your family, if it is not too painful to talk about."

"I will, but first we need to eat a real meal, not just sweets and tea. I will fetch some meat and butter from the stabbur and you can slice more bread that is under the towel on the table there." She threw a blanket around her shoulders and went outside. I hoped that I had not over-whelmed her with my story. And that she could be trusted. I felt a stab of guilt for never having confided in Runi or Agnas and Runa. They did not know that I was a fugitive, although I wonder if they suspected so. Now Dorthe knew more about me than anyone. How strange that I should confess everything upon just meeting her.

Dorthe came back then with food and we set to work preparing our meal. When we sat at the table to eat, she reached for my hand and said, "Let us thank God for our food. And that you are here." She started singing the traditional Norwegian prayer and I joined in, our voices blending. As soon as we reached the "Amen," Dorthe said, "Let us eat." I do not know if it was all the fresh air from the trip, or if it was the baring of my soul, but my appetite was huge. Everything tasted so good. I was embarrassed to eat so much, but Dorthe was unflustered. "You need to get some flesh on your bones. Believe me, you will earn your keep." She smiled so broadly, I could see the bread and butter between her teeth. I studied her face and what she saw in mine is what I saw in hers: Fadir's eyes. She also had my fadir's smile. My heart gave a little leap.

After our meal and the washing up, we again sat by the hearth. I retrieved my knitting and she mended a blanket. "So, now about my family. My brodir and his family lived in the house beyond the stabbur. He and his wife had three children, the oldest was four years." She put her mending on her lap and sighed. "They all died. Mor and Far also died last year of the pox. I am glad I did not know what last year would bring. I could not have bore it all had I known. I really thought some of them would survive. But we cared for each other until one by one, they were gone." She picked up her mending again, "It is a miracle, really, that I live." I found myself absently fingering the pock scars on my arm as she spoke. She took a few stitches and continued, "My Far was your Far's brodir. He

182

told me how sad he was when your far moved to Iceland. They were not just brodirs, but good friends, too. They had no other brors or sosters. My far was kind and jolly and he taught me so much. He loved to talk and he treated me like an adult in our conversations. My mor was more quiet. Once, while we were hanging laundry, she told me that she had lost three babies to stillbirth. I did not know what to say. You would know, since you have also lost a child." Dorthe looked at me and closed her eyes for a moment. My chest tightened with sadness. Then she continued, "She took good care of us. My bror and I never went to church without a bath and clean and mended clothes. She worked hard to make good food and warm coats and blankets." Dorthe held up the one she mended. "This is a blanket that she wove. But…" she paused, "I sensed a sadness in her. She mourned for her lost babies, I am sure, but she also seemed to have a yearning – maybe to do something besides being a wife and mother."

"Did she have special talents?" I asked.

"She had a beautiful singing voice and could pick up any instrument and play it. The church made use of her music, but maybe she wanted more."

I nodded. Maybe everyone everywhere wants more. I then asked, "Do you play any instruments?"

"Ja." She nodded toward the shelf where a fiddle rested. "I play some."

"I would love to hear you play sometime. Maybe you could teach me?" I was quick to add, "Of course, there is much work to do here. How have you managed all alone?"

Dorthe shook her head and chuckled, "People do not think a woman can run a homestead, and I have struggled some. After my family died, a neighbor offered to buy the homestead. I was not ready to part with it, and I did not take into account how hard it would be to keep up by myself.

Then two different men from the church came to propose marriage to me. I almost wondered if they had conferred on it, because one came right after the other. They both had pitiful sad-dog eyes and neither one inspired confidence nor romance in me. When I turned down the marriage offers, one of them accused me of being a half-wit. I guess not wanting just any man is considered illogical."

"Do you still see those men at church?"

"Oh, ja. The one is cordial enough; he has since married another maid and they are expecting a baby. The one who thinks I am half-witted avoids me. I take it as a game to make a point of speaking to him. I think it annoys him." She laughed. Then she became sober. "I did love a lad, though. I would have married that one, but he also died of the pox." She looked into the distance, then shook her head, "Maybe I am not destined to marry. It would be nice to have help, though…." Her voice trailed off.

"If you are inclined, tomorrow you can show me around and tell me what jobs you do not like to do and I will do them. I can work like a man," I said.

"That is a fine plan. First I will show you where you will sleep. My bed is in the nook here." She pointed to a place in the corner. "Mor and Far slept here and I slept in the loft. Before the pox," she added. "The loft is not being used; my old bed is up there."

"That will feel like home. I slept in the loft at home in Iceland."

"That is settled then. We will bring your pack up there and I will be sure you have what you need. No one has slept up there for a while. The blankets were cleaned when I washed the rest of the house after the pox."

"We had to burn much of the contents of Runi's bedroom after he died, especially his clothes and the bedding. Even the mattress was taken away and burned. It was required in the city because so many folks lived close to each other," I explained.

"That must have broken your heart, to not only lose him, but all of his things." We climbed the ladder to the loft.

"I still have something," I said. I rummaged in my pack until I found the wooden dog. "Runi made this for me."

Dorthe held it and said, "It is beautiful and well-loved, I see."

"I sleep with it in my hand every night."

She shook out the bedding and dust flew. Dorthe waved her hand and coughed. Then she lit the lamp on the bedside table. "You can put your things in this chest or hang them on these pegs. I will let you get settled. When you are ready, come back downstairs."

One by one, I took my belongings from my pack: the sling from Fadir, the note from Modir. I put them on a shelf above the bed. Birgir's carved wooden vegvisir stood propped in the corner, like a soldier standing guard. The blade from Tryggve rested on the bedside table, and the fishing net from Olav and the net bag from Runa hung on the pegs. Now I wished I had taken the angel that Runi carved for me but perhaps it was of comfort to Agnas and Runa. I put my clothes in the chest, out of sight. If I did not gain weight soon, I would alter them. As I turned to take the ladder back downstairs, I looked at the loft and it felt like home.

Downstairs, Dorthe had poured two glasses of amber liquid. She held one out to me. "Is it ale?" I asked.

"Whiskey. I found a jar of it hidden in the back of the cupboard. I thought I would save it for a special occasion." I took the glass and we clinked them together.

I took a gulp. Unlike bubbly ale or berry wine, the whiskey burned like hot soup down my throat. I held the glass high, "Skol!"

Dorthe took a sip and with a twinkle in her eye, she said, "You are a surprising maid. We will get along just fine."

The warmth of the spirits made its way to my belly and I took another sip. My eyes met Dorthe's and I began to giggle, then laugh and Dorthe did, too. We laughed uncontrolled until tears ran down our cheeks. Then we cried in earnest, like great storm clouds breaking. We sobbed, then sniffled, and drew in great hiccupping breaths. After some time, our tears were spent and our glasses were empty. My heart felt purged of its heavy grief. Finally, Dorthe took a deep breath and spoke, "Time for bed." I agreed.

CHAPTER 65

After a night of deep sleep, I woke to the sound of the door closing. I quickly went down the ladder to see Dorthe brushing off her coat. She stomped her boots. "We had a good amount of snow overnight."

"Why were you out so early?" I asked.

Dorthe chuckled. "I wanted to be sure that the stabbur and the other buildings were not too embarrassing to show you this morning. I have been a bit behind on some things, managing by myself. Let us have some breakfast and then we will get to work."

We downed some warm porridge and bundled up before going outside. Above the sound of the howling wind, I heard the bellwether then saw sheep approaching. "They are looking for food, I guess," I shouted.

Dorthe motioned for me to follow her and she produced the key for the stabbur. We climbed the steps, quickly went in and pushed the door closed. It was well stocked with hay for the animals and food for us as well. "How did you do this, all on your own?" I asked her.

"Truthfully, I do not know. A few people from the church helped me, but most of them are short of workers as well. It seems my life is full of miracles: a full stabbur, my health, and a new friend." She nudged me with her elbow.

We each gathered up as much hay as our arms could hold and went out to feed the sheep. Then I got another armload to bring to Dorthe's horse in the nearby shed while Dorthe locked the stabbur again. She then took me to the house that her brodir's family lived in. It was as if they had just stepped out, except that everything was covered in a fine layer of dust. "One of these days, we can put this house right. After everybody died, I just did not have the heart to tackle it."

Working on this homestead, doing familiar chores where my fadir grew up, was a strange comfort. I imagined things he may have done while here, like shooting the sling, riding the horse, getting hay from the stabbur. I learned that when he was young, Fadir shared the loft where I now slept with his brodir, Dorthe's far. And the horse that my fadir rode when he was a lad sired Dorthe's horse, Buttercup. All of these connections made me both glad and more and more homesick. I calculated that by summer, my three years of exile from Iceland would have passed. I could safely return home without worrying about Einar's retribution for Pjetur's death. I began to dream about going back to Bergen to see Anna, then to the Faroe Islands to visit Agnas and Runa where I would retrieve Raven. Then I would return home to Iceland. The longer I worked at Dorthe's homestead, the more the idea of leaving became real.

I claimed Dorthe's brodir's neglected house as my special project and worked there between my regular chores. Dorthe left me to it, keeping to her own house and its chores. I had cleaned and purged the house room by room until I got to the bedroom shared by Dorthe's brodir and his wife. I stripped the bed and made a pile to wash, then opened the drawers holding their clothes. Dorthe happened to arrive just then. "Lara! Look what wonders you have done here! Where are you?"

"In the bedroom," I replied. I was holding a pair of trousers up to myself when Dorthe entered the room. I felt a little sheepish, and quickly folded the trousers over my arm.

"Wait," Dorthe said. "What was that?"

I laughed a little, uncomfortably. Then I explained, "When I was in the Faroe Islands, my systir Runa got me to wear lads' clothing from time to time. I wore them again in Skien when I was at the ironworks. I guess I was just thinking about that when I saw your brodir's trousers."

"Wonderful idea. Why have I never thought to try that?" Dorthe grabbed the trousers and kicked off her boots. Then she sat on the bed, pulled the trousers on, and held up her skirt. "Look at that! Do I leave my skirt on or take it off?"

"We just wore the trousers with a tunic and, if the weather was cold, a coat," I explained.

Dorthe quickly untied her skirt and let it drop to the floor. She kicked it onto the laundry pile and spun around. Her apron flew out like a sail. She untied it and threw it onto the pile, too. "Ha!" she said. "If we are working like men, we will dress the part. Surely there is another pair of trousers for you." She began to rummage through the drawers and triumphantly held up a pair. "For you," she said.

I laughed and put them on. We strutted around the room like roosters. "Woman, you are a half-wit," Dorthe said in a deep, pompous voice.

"And you must marry me, even though I am an ass," I replied in an equally deep voice.

We fell onto the bed, laughing, until I jumped up, "I have to visit the outhouse. Too much laughing!" I ran from the house without a coat.

We wore our men's clothes when we worked around the homestead from then on. Dorthe said that it made her feel free. But each Sunday we put on our maid's skirts and best aprons and took Buttercup and the small wagon to the ancient white Bo church. Dorthe made a point of introducing me to the lad who called her "half-wit." We could not look at each other during the sermon or giggles would overtake us. Disapproving glares from fellow parishioners made us giggle even more. The altar table was painted with an Eye of God. That big eye watching us should have had a calming influence, but it did not.

After the church service on Christmas Eve, we greeted the preacher at the door, and I complimented him on his sermon. He said, "If you and Dorthe wait until I am done here, I have something for you from the missus and me." We milled around the back of the church like sheep in the yard waiting for hay. The preacher visited with all the old matrons and men and patted the children on the head. Finally, he closed the door and turned to us, beaming. "Come," he beckoned us to his tiny, unheated office. He opened his desk drawer and produced a tall jar. "You cannot have a proper joyous yuletide without traditional Christmas beer," he said. "Here. Drink it in good health." I took the jar and tucked it under my arm.

"Tusen takk," Dorthe said. "If you and your wife are out by our homestead, please stop in for a visit."

When we returned home, we put a bundle of grain out by the barn door as a Christmas gift for the birds. Then I began a letter to Bestemor and Bestefar, letting them know that we were well and that I would be ready to return to them as soon as the weather allowed. As we sipped on the Jul beer, I told Dorthe of my plan to return to Skien, and then go to the Faroe Islands and on to Iceland, timing my summer arrival to coincide with the end of my three-year exile. Dorthe finished her beer and set down the cup. She said, "You have not kept your intention to return to Iceland a secret. I understand why you want to go home. Maybe you can send a different letter to your family in Skien." I looked at her with questioning brows and she continued, "Do not answer now, but would you consider taking me with you? I could sell the homestead."

CHAPTER 66

The neighbor whose land adjoined Dorthe's had offered to buy her farmstead and now she went to see him with the intention of finding out what he could pay. His growing family had somehow escaped being decimated by the epidemic and he wanted to offer his adult married children homes of their own. Adding Dorthe's land and buildings to his own would double his homestead. They worked out a fair price and the timing of the sale. Bestemor and Bestefar would not have to come to fetch me; Dorthe and I would take Dorthe's wagon pulled by Buttercup to Skien when the weather broke.

Only the most precious possessions would make the trip with us. We spent any spare moments sorting and packing. "What about this?" I held up the family Bible.

"Of course, I will take that. All of our family records are written in the Bible. Look here," she took the black leather-bound book and turned crinkly pages. "This is my Far's handwriting, and his Mor's before him." She pointed to the pages titled Births and Marriages. There I saw my fadir's birth listed and the marriage of my Modir and Fadir. Then she turned to the page titled Deaths. "I added my family members as each one passed." She traced the words with her finger. "Seeing the young children's names make me most sad."

"Ja," I said, "Lives cut short." I wondered again about how Modir, Fadir, and little Ole fared. My determination to return home strengthened as we continued our preparations. "Do you have anything that I could bring to Fadir? Maybe something of his parents or brodir, your far?"

She considered, then jumped up, "Ja." She rummaged in a drawer and produced a pocketknife. "I remember Bestefar using this knife." She pulled the blade out from the handle. "He was always sure to keep it sharpened. See how thin the blade has become. Far said he learned to carve from Bestefar using this. Take it." She carefully folded in the blade and then pressed the smooth wood into my palm. "Perhaps Bestefar taught your Far to whittle and carve with it, too."

"Takk," I said. I thought of Runi's carvings. Fadir would have liked Runi.

After many gray, timeless winter days, signs of spring slowly emerged. The lengthening morning light took on a warmer slant and I had to squint, unaccustomed to the bright light after so many gloomy days. The darkness of night came later and later, and we welcomed the extra time to work without candlelight or oil lamps. Large drifts of snow turned to big puddles of mud, caking the fleece of the sheep and Buttercup's hoofs. Before the lambing, the neighbor who would soon assume ownership of them did the shearing, but according to their agreement, that year's wool profits went to Dorthe. When morning frost no longer collected on the horse paths, we determined that it was time to leave.

The people of the church had a going-away party for us after the Sunday service. Everyone brought favorite dishes and we all shared a bountiful meal. Afterwards, Dorthe played her fiddle and some of the others joined in with fiddles and wooden flutes. The preacher drummed on a wooden box to keep time. Some of the older folks sang and the little children danced. We were given gifts: a blanket, a carved wooden cheese box with a large wheel of cheese inside, and two wooden spoons. Congratulatory handshakes were offered both to us and to the neighbor who bought Dorthe's homestead.

The night before our departure, we had everything packed and the neighbor arrived with the money for the purchase of Dorthe's homestead. He counted, she counted, I counted, until we were all satisfied and Dorthe wrote out a letter granting ownership to the neighbor. After he left, Dorthe and I sat by the fire, as we had become accustomed to in the evenings, and we finished off the contents of the whiskey jar, sipping in silence. Finally, Dorthe spoke. "I was a bit sad about leaving my home until now. I thought I would feel heavy-hearted tonight, but instead I feel as if a big weight has been lifted from me. I am still young, with my whole life to live."

"Ja," I agreed. "As my friend Runa would say, 'We will have fun.'"

Dorthe said, "And I will meet your friends..."

"... and my family in Iceland," I added.

"We should go to sleep now so that morning will come sooner," Dorthe said.

"Skol!" I finished my drink in a big gulp.

"Skol!"

One last time, I climbed up to the loft and into my bed. I looked at my full pack; it was ready to go, and so was I.

With morning light, Buttercup stood patiently waiting while we loaded the wagon. The neighbor arrived to feed the sheep that now belonged to him. "Good travels," he said. He patted Buttercup's nose, then he and his adult son went to their wagon and began bringing their furniture and clothes into the house.

Under her breath, Dorthe said to me, "Well, they are certainly not wasting any time taking over. But..." she patted her bodice, "I have all the money sewn right here. That makes leaving even easier."

She climbed onto the wagon seat and I followed. She shook the reins, and made a chuk-chuk sound. "On, Buttercup," she said, and without a backward glance, we took the path to Skien.

CHAPTER 67
RETURN TO SKIEN NORWAY

The day proved pleasant with sunshine and a mild breeze. The preacher had drawn us a map of our journey, and we spread it on the bench between us, looking at it whenever there was a fork in the path. Buttercup kept up a steady pace and we arrived at Bestemor and Bestefar's homestead in time for the mid-day meal. When we approached the house, I heard a child squeal and then all the family members converged on the wagon to greet us. Lars took Buttercup from the wagon and led her to the shed where she would be fed and watered, and the others helped to unload the wagon. Bestemor stood on the porch with a big smile, directing where the bundles and boxes should go. Bestefar introduced Dorthe to the family members. Sara remembered her from visits to Bo church, but most did not. The little girls took Dorthe's hands and led her to Sara and Knud's house where we would eat our meal. Bestemor put her arm around my waist and we walked together to Sara's house. "Seeing you today puts a bloom in my heart," Bestemor said. "How we have missed you!"

"I missed you, too." I leaned over and kissed her cheek.

Over lunch, excited faces learned of our time at Dorthe's and then their expressions turned to surprise when she revealed that she had sold the homestead. Bestefar said, "I am sure you considered it carefully before you made that big decision. I wonder if you should have had a man help you with negotiating the price."

Bestemor slapped his arm, "Dorthe and Lara are more than capable."

Bestefar leaned back and looked at Bestemor from beneath his bushy brows, "I was only saying…."

"Ja. Only saying. The deal is done. They made their price and surely the neighbor did not take advantage of them."

"He bought the land, the buildings, the contents, and the livestock, all priced separately and fairly," I said.

Dorthe looked from Bestefar to Bestemor, "My far and mor would have approved," she said finally. An uncomfortable silence fell over the room.

Sara stood and began clearing dishes. "To celebrate Lara's return and Dorthe's arrival, I have some sweets."

The children bounced in their seats and everyone breathed and smiled, the brief conflict resolved. Sometimes I think that the Vikings' love of fighting wore us out for conflict. As a people, we are uncomfortable when disagreements arise and like to put things right quickly. I wonder if other peoples are like that, too. I was grateful that Sara broke the tension and the sweets were a welcome surprise.

The rest of the afternoon at Sara and Knud's house was spent visiting and catching up, and then we returned to Bestemor and Bestefar's house. That evening, sitting by the fire with Bestemor and Bestefar, we brought out the gifts from the church. "I would like for you to keep the cheese box and blanket," Dorthe said. "It will be hard to travel with bulky and heavy things. Lara and I will each keep one of the wooden spoons."

Bestemor unfolded and admired the blanket, then draped it over the chair. "Lovely. I will slice some of the cheese now for our evening meal. Takk, Dorthe." She stood, then turned, "You said travel. Are you going away?"

Dorthe looked at me. She had not meant to bring up our plans yet; she knew I would want to gently break the news that we were not staying. I took a deep breath, then said, "We will stay for a short time and then we are making our way to my home in Iceland by way of the Faroe Islands."

"Nei!" Bestefar threw his hands in the air. "Two maids traveling alone? And on the sea? Nei."

I put my hand on Dorthe's arm when I could see that she had the impulse to disagree with Bestefar. Bestemor still stood with the cheese, her mouth open in disbelief. "Leaving us? I thought Dorthe was joining our family. And we must share a late Jul celebration. Surely you can stay through the summer months, at least."

Dorthe and I exchanged glances. "May we talk about this after we eat and have a good night's sleep? I have missed sleeping under your roof and sharing meals with you," I said.

Bestemor's sense of hospitality took over. "Ja. We can talk tomorrow. Tonight you need food and sleep." She bustled away to prepare supper.

Bestefar continued to glower at us, moving his disapproving gaze from Dorthe to me and back to Dorthe. He took out his pipe and tapped tobacco into it. "Your bestemor is content to wait to talk, so I will also. But this is not over," he said. He lit the pipe and took a long draw.

I stood, "Come, Dorthe, we will help Bestemor with the food." Dorthe quickly stood and we left Bestefar to his smoke, which I hoped would offer him some calming comfort. I remembered the strong opinions he expressed about my wearing men's clothes and working with metal before I left for Dorthe's. His judgements never seemed far from his tongue. Perhaps old age makes a person more opinionated and unafraid to express those opinions. I did not have protective grandparents to fuss over me until I came to Norway. Although it was nice to know that they cared so much, I was used to being independent. And poor Dorthe. Surely she did not expect to be chided and thwarted by my grandparents when she came here with me. Uff da.

CHAPTER 68

A silent supper was followed by terse goodnights and Dorthe and I retired to my bedroom where we were surrounded by our belongings. On seeing the bulk of the piles, I realized that we would need to do some more sorting before embarking on the next leg of our journey. As soon as I closed and latched the door, Dorthe blew the hair from her brow with a loud puff. "Getting away from your grandparents may be the most difficult part of our journey," she said.

I chuckled and then we both began to giggle until Bestemor knocked on the door. "Is everything all right in there?" she asked.

I choked out, "We are fine, Bestemor" and Dorthe snorted which made us both laugh even more. Finally, we sniffled as we readied ourselves for bed.

Dorthe rolled up an extra blanket and put it in the center of the bed. "I am not used to sharing a bed," she explained. "This will help me not to kick you in my sleep."

"Takk for that," I said. "Since we have had to tell Bestemor and Bestefar about our plans already, I think we should tell the rest of the family tomorrow. I would like to tell them myself."

"Good luck with that," Dorthe said.

"Ja. I think we may have some allies in our cause among my fetters. And Bestefar's bluster is not lasting. He will come around, I am quite sure."

"Say your prayers, Lara. And I will say mine."

CHAPTER 69

Bestemor had our breakfast porridge waiting when we emerged, sleepy-eyed, the next morning. "The porridge would be warmer if you had gotten up earlier," she said with her back to us. She made work of something at the stove, clearly avoiding talk about our plans to leave. Bestefar was not as reticent and while we were still eating, he came through the door full of bluster and determination.

"I see you are awake," he said. He hung up his coat and hat, then continued. "I was down at Sara and Knud's, telling them of your plans." He frowned and hesitated, "I cannot believe they are taking your part, but they think we should allow you to go." Dorthe and I exchanged glances. She smiled briefly before she looked down at her bowl. When I kept quiet, he continued. "They seem to think you have already been through a lot and have survived, so you will also survive this long trip." He took a deep breath and blew out his cheeks. "What can I say? You are not children. I guess I must swallow some camels."

Bestemor cleared our bowls and spoons from the table and brought tea. Bestefar continued, "I do not often take back my words, but we know you want to go home."

"Although we would prefer that you thought of this place as your home," Bestemor said.

Bestefar nodded and sat on the bench next to me. He covered my hand with his. Now his voice was gentle, "We are afraid we will never see you again." I closed my eyes and a tear escaped. I knew how they felt. I wished that all my loved ones could be in one place. All together. Always.

Bestemor rested her hand on my shoulder. "We will not make the same mistake with you as we did with your mor and far. You have our blessing." She then sat across from me with her cup of tea.

We all sniffled and then sipped our tea in silence for a while. Finally, Bestefar said, "Knud has something for you. When we go to their house for mid-day meal he can give it to you."

"What is it?" I asked.

"He wants to show you himself. I do not want to spoil the surprise."

Dorthe suddenly spoke. "We love surprises."

CHAPTER 7◊

As we walked to Sara and Knud's house later, we passed the stabbur. I noticed that the door was left ajar. "Bestefar," I said, "Is someone in the stabbur?"

"I will check later. Now we do not want to be late for Sara's meal. She does not tolerate that well," Bestefar replied.

Bestemor coughed behind her hand, but I could see that she was hiding a laugh.

All the family had already gathered and was waiting for us. The house was decorated with fir boughs. "Gud Jul!" They shouted as we entered. The children, dressed in white robes, sang the Santa Lucia song. One of the little girls wore the traditional candle-lit wreath on her head.

"Oh, lovely!" Dorthe exclaimed, clapping her hands.

Bestemor said, "Since you missed Yuletide with the family, we thought to make a feast for you now."

I was overcome by all the attention and generosity. Such a lavish celebration. We feasted on fish and beef, potatoes and biscuits, vegetables and fruit. "I am stuffed." I exclaimed.

"Wait until you see the dessert," Lars said.

Knud leaned back in his chair, "I declare no more working today; we are having a holiday."

Dorthe said, "I will need a nap after all of this feasting."

"We will no doubt all be drowsy," Sara said "All except the children, of course. After eating sweets for dessert, they will be full of energy." We all laughed and the children bounced in their seats.

Knud continued, "We will have our rice pudding and then we will give Lara her gifts."

Gifts? I was already feeling embarrassed about all the expense and attention. Although I was full, I did not hesitate to eat the delicious, creamy dessert and when that was done, ginger cookies were passed on a china plate. Of course, I had to have a cookie or two as well, and then coffee.

"And now," Knud said, "Lara, please come sit here. We want to see you open your gifts."

I obediently sat in Knud's large chair by the hearth. First, Bestemor brought a package. "Every respectable Norwegian woman must have a bunad. This is yours." I opened the wrapping to reveal a black skirt, embroidered near the hem, a white apron with floral trim, an embroidered bodice with silver clasps, a bonnet similarly adorned, and a pair of black shoes with silver buckles. My eyes grew larger with every piece of clothing I unfolded.

"Oh, I love it. I will go and put it on right now," I said.

"Wait. There is more," Sara said.

Knud handed me a decorative purse that attached to the bunad's waistband. "Look inside," he said.

I took the bag that was unexpectedly heavy. I twisted the clasp and the hinge fell open to reveal coins. "What is this?" I asked.

Knud chuckled, "Money, of course. The jewelry you made fetched a good price, as I promised. Bestefar added a few, too. And here, I saved this." In my palm he placed the wide silver ring with carving that I had made. "It seemed meant for your finger," he said. I slowly slid the ring on my finger. My fingers were thinner when I made the ring and it would no longer fit over my knuckle to cover my wedding tattoo. I was actually relieved about that. I slipped it easily onto my little finger and held up my hand to admiring Oooohs and Aaahhhs.

"One last gift," Bestefar said. He approached me looking somewhat bashful, and fumbled in his vest pocket for a bit, then produced a key. "This fits the lock on our stabbur. We want you to always know you have a home here. What is ours is yours."

"Here," Dorthe said, "Let me help you tie it on your belt."

I stood and watched as the key dropped from the end of the belt onto my skirt. If I never had wife keys, I would always have this one. I looked at the beaming faces of my family. "How can I thank you?"

Bestefar put his arm around my shoulder and said, "Knowing you are in the world is enough."

CHAPTER 71

The days that followed were filled with re-packing, playing with the children, and conversing with my family. Dorthe fell in with everyone as if she had always been a part of the family. She and I rested and relaxed, letting the others fuss over us, knowing we would only be there a short time. When, after a few days, we determined that we were ready to head to Porsgrunn and on to Bergen, we had one last family meal together. Everyone wore their traditional Norwegian clothing as if we were attending an important church service or a wedding. Dorthe had brought along her bunad, which was nice, but not nearly as fancy and fine as my new one. I felt like a queen wearing such finery and carrying money of my own. What a feeling of freedom that afforded me. Dorthe asked Knud if, after taking us to the ship, the family would look after her horse Buttercup and keep her wagon, and of course, he was happy to oblige.

Once again, I had to steel my heart for a tearful farewell. Bestemor and Bestefar put on brave faces, but then we all hugged and cried. My hankie was soggy by the time I climbed into the back of the wagon with our full packs. Dorthe sat in the driver's seat for one last trip with Buttercup. Knud would drive the horse and wagon back after we were delivered to the ship. It seemed fitting that I rode backwards in the wagon, watching the family, then the farmstead, then the village grow smaller and farther away. As soon as we were out of sight of the familiar places, I felt my heart turn to my next destination. The thought of seeing Anna, Agnas, Runa and then my Iceland family and friends created a strange pulling in my chest. Leaving was hard, but going was exciting.

CHAPTER 72
SKIEN TO PORSGRUNN TO BERGEN NORWAY

The same ship that brought me from Bergen to Porsgrunn was the one we boarded to return to Bergen. I felt comfortable in the familiar surroundings and showed Dorthe where our cabin was and the dining room. How wonderful it was for the two of us, independent young women, traveling with our own money. Dorthe spun around on the top deck with her arms outstretched. She said, "I had never before left Bo, and already I have been to Skien and Porsgrunn. I could get used to being a world traveler."

The trip to Bergen took us to the same ports I had visited with Bestemor and Bestefar, so I enjoyed showing Dorthe around and told her the things that my grandparents had shared with me about the stops. In the evenings, flashing beacons on the mountainsides along the coast drew us along. During meals, we sat with different couples on a holiday or visiting family. By the time we arrived in Bergen, we had made new friends. Dorthe's easy, outgoing nature made it easier for me to join in. Following her example, I found that I could carry on a conversation with most folks. It seemed that if I were friendly and talkative, they were, too.

Our arrival at the port in Bergen suddenly filled me with dread. Seeing the buildings lining the wharf flooded my heart and mind with memories of Runi, and I felt the loss of him more deeply there than I had in months. Standing on the deck with the happy crowds of travelers waving to waiting friends and families filled me with loneliness. My chest felt tight and my head hurt from holding back tears. Without prompting, Dorthe quietly reached out and held my hand, still looking at the pier. We watched the men secure the heavy ropes and lower the heavy, groaning gangway, and then it was time to go. Without exchanging a word, we gathered our packs and left the ship.

We passed the place of the pox victims' pyre, the tavern where Runi and I shared that most wonderful meal, and came to the blue house with white trim at the end of the row. "Here we are," I said.

"This is Anna's house, then," Dorthe said. I nodded. I hesitated. Dorthe asked, "Do you want me to open the door, or do you want to do it?"

"I can do it," I said. I lifted the familiar latch and opened the door, expecting to see Anna behind her reception desk. Instead, a tall distinguished-looking gentleman stood there. I was caught off guard. "Who are you?" I asked.

The man cleared his throat and looked at us from behind glittering spectacles, "May I help you?" he asked.

"Wha – Where is Anna?" I asked.

"Why do you ask?"

"I expected to see her here. I am her friend Lara." I turned to Dorthe, "And this is my fetter Dorthe."

His brows shot up and his face brightened. "Lara! I have heard so much about you! Anna will be back shortly. She went to the market. Was she expecting you?"

"Nei. We are passing through, but hoped to see her and perhaps spend the night. Are you … her husband?" I asked.

The man threw his head back and laughed. "I am her bror, Arne. I can get a room for you and she will be here soon."

"Takk, Arne," I said. He motioned with a key for us to follow him upstairs where he bypassed Runi's room and took us to the end of the hall. "You are sharing a room?" he asked.

"Ja," we said in unison. The room had two small beds; Dorthe would not need to roll up a blanket to separate us here.

We dropped our packs and Arne said, "I will be downstairs if you need anything. I will tell Anna that you are here as soon as she returns." With that, he set the key on a small table, turned, and shut the door behind him.

Dorthe and I fumbled in our packs for a bit and then she said, "Being here has to be so hard for you."

"Ja," I said, "But I could not come to Bergen and not stay with Anna. I am eager for you two to meet."

"This was not Runi's room, I hope," Dorthe looked around.

"Nei. It is at the top of the stairs." I could not help but peek in Runi's room as we had passed it. The open door revealed that it looked entirely different than how I had left it. The walls had been painted and all the furniture rearranged, with different bedding and curtains. I had the sudden thought that Anna needed to clear those sad memories from her life, too.

I sighed. "I think we could both use a little something. Come with me to the tavern."

Dorthe laughed, "Lead the way."

We told Arne we would return soon when we passed him on our way out. He smiled and waved, barely looking up from the maps spread out on the desk.

We linked arms and walked up the street. Now that I had revisited the house where Runi died, and lived through being there again, I began to feel like a strong, independent woman once more. I wondered if returning to the tavern would stir up more sad memories, but I was happy to be there with Dorthe. I felt like I had conquered a steep mountain and was now in a more pleasant valley. We ordered bread and ale and listened to loud voices speaking in strange languages. I told Dorthe what Runi had told me about the countries represented in the tavern. "I am simply amazed," she said, "I feel like I am traveling around the world when I am just sitting right here. With you. Drinking ale. Amazing." She chewed her bread and looked around with wide eyes.

Soon we walked back to Anna's house, feeling full and light-headed. As we approached, the door flew open and Anna ran to me and swept me in her arms. "Oh, my dear girl. You have returned."

I kissed her cheek. "Yes, and I brought my fetter, Dorthe."

"Lovely, lovely," Anna said. "I am sorry I was not here to greet you." She ushered us in the door. "Come in, come in."

During supper shared with her bror Arne, we learned some of his story. He was a ship's captain in port for some minor repairs. He would be leaving soon to bring lumber and ore to the Faroe Islands and then he would continue on with shipments for Iceland. Of course, we asked if we could travel with him, and he was obliging. We negotiated a price and made arrangements to leave with him in a few days. He and Dorthe carried on lively conversation while Anna and I ate quietly, and then cupped our chins in our hands and looked at each other across the table. We had been through so much together. It seemed like a dream to be sitting with Anna once again. She pulled from her bodice the silver pendant from Bestemor and Bestefar, and I held out mine. She reached for my arm and pushed up my sleeve, and I did the same to hers. We lay our pock-scarred arms next to each other on the table. I felt the warmth of her soft skin as the Captain and Dorthe talked on and on.

⟨HAPTER 73

"How wonderful that Anna's bror can take us on his ship," Dorthe exclaimed as we readied ourselves for bed after supper. "How providential."

"Ja," I agreed. "You two certainly had a lot to talk about."

"He has had such a fascinating life. His wife died of the pox. Did you hear that part? He has no children. He is quite a bit younger than Anna, I think." Dorthe was even more animated than usual. She unfolded and folded the same shift three times. Then she dug deep in her pack and pulled out a pair of trousers. "Look what I brought," she said. "I hope you brought yours, too. We should wear them on the ship. We can cause a stir, maybe."

I pulled my trousers out and waved them like a flag. "We certainly could wear them when we arrive on the Faroe Islands. It would be a fitting tribute to Runa to arrive in the clothes she prefers."

"Ja. I think so. We will do that," Dorthe nodded dramatically.

While waiting for the ship to be ready, we helped Anna some with meals and cleaning, but mostly we sat at tables on the cobblestone streets in front of the buildings of the traders, the German Hanseatic League, and tried to guess what the men were discussing in their foreign tongues. Men argued loudly all day, smoking pipes and drinking. We could guess only a few words that were similar to Norsk, so we entertained ourselves by inventing dialogue to explain their gestures and facial expressions. Our laughter increased with the ale we drank. "You have a face like a cod and breath like burnt eggs," Dorthe said in a self-important voice.

"Your wife has big feet," I replied, hooking my thumbs in my bodice.

"You eat like a donkey."

"You drink like a whale, and look like one, too."

We attracted stares from a nearby table, and soon a burly man wearing a waistcoat and pocket-chain stood behind Dorthe's chair, leaned down, and blew pipe smoke in her face. "Was ist so lustig?"

Dorthe leaned in and whispered loudly, "Did he say 'lust'?"

I whispered back, "I think he did."

Loud throat clearing made us both turn. Arne had his hand on the man's shoulder. He spoke to him in German. We did not know exactly what he said, but waistcoat man backed away and went to his table. Arne drew up a chair. "May I join you?" he asked.

"Takk for making that man go away," Dorthe said.

He sat and waved away her words. "You would have handled it. I came to see you with news."

"What news?" I asked.

Arne motioned for a beer, leaned back, and stretched out his long legs. His polished black shoes reflected the sunlight. "The ship is ready to sail. We leave in the morning." A cup of ale arrived for Arne.

Dorthe raised her cup with a broad smile. "To a good voyage," she exclaimed.

Arne and I raised ours, too. "To a good voyage," we said.

And then the three of us spent our late afternoon together, laughing and talking on the Bergen pier. If anyone had told me that I would find any joy in this place, I would not have believed it. But Bestemor was right. As time passed, my grief was a bit easier.

That evening, as Dorthe and Arne talked, I helped Anna with the supper washing up. She handed me a plate and in a low voice asked, "Have you heard from our friend, Hildur lately?" She glanced at me.

"She appeared to me with my Iceland family in dreams a few times, but I have not had those dreams recently. You?"

Anna slowly worked the cloth around the rim of a bowl. "Ja. She showed me a wedding. The groom may have been my bror."

CHAPTER 74

When morning arrived, Dorthe and I cleaned our room for Anna. We left coins on the table. I knew she would not accept anything for our stay if we tried to pay her. As we passed Captain Arne's room, we saw that the door was open and his things were gone. Struck with panic that he had left without us, we scurried down the stairs and saw his satchel waiting by the door. He and Anna were visiting over a cup of coffee. It appeared that he had already eaten. Anna looked up and smiled when we entered the room, "I have prepared some biscuits and jam for you to take with you. Arne is eager to push off."

"We should have gotten up earlier," I said.

"Takk for biscuits," Dorthe said.

The Captain stood. "Anna, we will be on our way, then."

I quickly wrote down the location of the farm in Iceland for Anna so that we could write to each other. She clutched the slip of paper in her hand and we embraced each other, neither of us wanting to let go. Finally Arne coughed and Dorthe patted my arm. "We need to go. Takk, Anna, for your hospitality and friendship."

I had hoped for a pretty day, but the weather was drizzly and fog hung in the harbor like an old, dirty blanket. Arne led the way with his satchel in one hand and rolled up charts and maps under his arm. As we approached the ship, crew members shouted "Ahoy" and waved. Once again, I walked up a gangway and onto a ship.

This ship was unlike the Dutch trading vessel that Runi and I took on our journey from the Faroe Islands to Norway. Fresh black paint gleamed from the trim and masts. Nets and ropes were neatly coiled and stacked. Sails showed some sign of repair but were whole and sturdy. The wood of the deck was wet from the rain, but it was clear that they had been recently swabbed. No mud or grime anywhere. I marveled that we made it across the wild North Sea in the other vessel after seeing this one.

Arne's face reflected his pride in his vessel. He took pleasure in Dorthe's exclamations of admiration. "Follow me. I will show you the cabin you will share. I hope you do not mind, the cabin has no porthole, but it will be dark and quiet for sleeping."

He led us to the stern of the ship, directly above the keel and rudder where his quarters were located. He set his satchel and the rolls on a table and then swept us back out to steps that led one deck below. I hoped we would get another chance to see his quarters. The gleaming wood and instruments fascinated me. As we climbed down the steps, Dorthe asked, "Will you show us how you navigate the ship? Might we join you in your quarters sometime?" Arne did not answer. Our affable, easy-going companion of the day before was now all business.

He opened a door to reveal a cozy interior cabin with two small bunks. "This cabin is generally occupied by an officer. My second mate is bunking with another sailor for our trip." We set our packs on the beds and hurried to follow Arne who was already headed down a narrow hallway. "Come, I will show you the rest of the ship quickly and then we must be off." He led us to the dining hall, introduced us to the cook and his first mate, and showed us where the cargo was loaded. "We are a fully loaded vessel on this trip," he said. "I may not have much time to spend with you. My attention must go to the safe arrival of the people and goods on the ship."

"Of course," Dorthe blushed. "I did not mean to be impertinent."

"Believe me, I would prefer to drink ale and visit with you maids, but my holiday is over. Back to work. Please excuse me." With that, he turned and began shouting orders to the crew. The familiar sounds of the men working in harmony to launch the ship filled the deck. Dorthe and I watched the men work then I felt the surge of the ship as it moved away from the wharf. I looked toward Anna's house. There she was, at the door, waving a white hankie in the fog.

⟨HAPTER 75
THE NORTH SEA

I had thought there might be other passengers on the ship, but Dorthe and I were the only ones. The sailors were courteous to us, but not friendly. The Captain must have given orders. The voyage would have been dull if not for Dorthe. She taught me a game with an improvised board and game pieces that involved complicated moves of dried beans, coins, and buttons she named king, queen, pawn, and others. She won every game and whooped loudly each time until I began to learn the strategy. Then it was my turn to gloat. We read Dorthe's Bible and I spent time on the deck during fair weather, breathing the fresh sea air and thinking about what I might face in the Faroe Islands. Modir always told me not to borrow trouble, meaning that I should not worry about what might not happen. But might it not also be true that anticipating woe could make accepting it easier? I would have to tell Agnas and Runa about Runi first of all, knowing their hearts would be broken.

Dorthe milled around the captain's quarters. Finally, on a day when the seas were calm and winds favorable, he invited us to join him in his quarters for our mid-day meal while the first mate took over his duties. He showed us the ship's log where he wrote down the conditions of the seas and skies, the position of the ship, and the status of the cargo, crew, and vessel. The book had entries from when he first began to sail as captain years prior to this voyage. "I started out on the crew, as most sailors do, and when I received my inheritance, I bought this ship. Anna bought the boarding house, and our oldest bror emigrated. We never heard where he went. We were not close."

He showed us his compass and let us peer through his spyglass. Dorthe turned and looked at me with it and exclaimed, "Lara! Your eye is huge!" I was bewitched watching the sand run through his large hourglass. The sea charts we had seen him carry onto the ship were spread out onto a table. He spoke of sailing by the stars and explained that the lines on the chart indicated water depths. While he and Dorthe were still bent over the charts, I was drawn to the large map that hung on the wall. I had never seen the shape of countries before. Norway was long and narrow. I found Bergen. Skien was not marked but I saw the waterway that lead inland from Porsgrunn. The Faroe Islands were much smaller than I had imagined, and there was Iceland. My finger traced its outline and I found the fjord near my home.

Arne looked over my shoulder. "We will be docking in Akureyri," he pointed to the northern port city at the base of a long fjord.

"My home is not so far from there," I replied.

"Do you think we will be able to find someone to transport us to Lara's home?" Dorthe asked.

"I am quite sure. Akureyri is nearly as busy a port as Bergen."

"Takk for food, Arne," I said. "Please excuse me." I descended the ladder to our cabin and quietly closed the door. My meal threatened to come up. Either I was seasick or looking at the map stirred my anxiety. I was suddenly afraid to go home. I lay on the bed in the darkness. What if Einar or the Master did not obey the law and tried to hurt me when I returned? What if they had hurt my family while I was away? Was I putting Dorthe in danger, too? What might the pox have done to those I loved in the Faroe Islands and at home? My head pounded. I closed my eyes and thankfully drifted off to sleep.

A triangle of light fell across my face when Dorthe opened the door. She quietly closed it and ran into something with a loud bang. "Faen!" she whispered. Her bed creaked when she lay down. "Lara?" she whispered, "Are you asleep?"

"Not any more," I said. I had to smile. How could I answer if I were asleep?

"After you left, Arne said he could help us hire a wagon to take us to your home in Iceland, and he said if things were going well with the ship, he might accompany us. He is such a nice man. I think his glasses make him look intelligent. Of course, he is intelligent, or he could not be the captain of a ship." She took a breath and continued, "We shared a glass of ale and talked for a long time. Were you asleep all that time?"

I smiled in the dark. "Ja. I was feeling a little seasick. I am better now."

"Arne said he thought that might be the case and said it would be best to let you rest. He is back to work now. He said to listen for the ships bells. They ring every four hours and after two bells, a working shift is over. Then the rest of the crew – not the captain, of course -- rotates to take breaks. He said if the seas cooperate, he would have us join him again." Her bed creaked and her clothes rustled. "I am not really tired. I just wanted to check on you."

"I think some fresh air would feel good. Should we go up on deck?" I asked.

CHAPTER 76
TORSHAVN TO KIRKJUBOUR FAROE ISLANDS

The shrieks and screams of the soaring, diving gray and white fulmars signaled approaching land. A shout from the crow's nest confirmed it. We were nearing Torshavn. My heart pounded as the harbor came into focus. The ship anchored and smaller boats began to approach to fetch the cargo. We quickly changed into our trousers, gathered all of our belongings, and waited on deck for Arne. He had promised to take us to shore as soon as he was sure things were secure on the ship.

Seeing the cluster of buildings and the rocky outcropping reminded me of the time Runa and I spent there at the Faroese Althing. Runi was still alive then. I wondered if I would mark time that way for the rest of my life: while Runi was alive and after Runi died. We were engrossed in watching the cargo being hoisted onto the boats and did not notice when Arne joined us. Surprised, Dorthe jumped and laughed. "Oh, you," she said and playfully nudged Arne's elbow.

"You maids surprise me," he said, looking at our trousers. "I should have put you 'lads' on my crew."

We laughed and followed him. When we turned around and climbed down the ladder I was glad of the trousers and Dorthe said, "Lara, this was the best idea. We will not worry about skirts this way."

When we arrived on the shore, I saw a figure in a black suit and hat standing by a wagon. The horse and wagon looked familiar. As I walked closer I recognized the preacher. "Dorthe, wait here," I said.

I approached him and tapped his arm. His bushy eyebrows shot up, "Lara. Is that you?"

"Ja. I am back," I said.

"Are you going to Runa's?" he asked. I nodded and he continued, "I am here to fetch a load of lumber. I can give you a ride."

I pointed to Dorthe. "Will there be room for my fraendi Dorthe, too?"

"Ja, sure. See me when the lumber has been loaded."

I told Dorthe that we had a ride to Kirkjubour. Arne said, "Be back here tomorrow by mid-day. We leave for Iceland then."

The preacher waved when the lumber had been loaded and we climbed onto the wagon. I sat on the bench with the preacher and Dorthe sat in the wagon on the lumber. I was glad for her sake that it was not a long trip. That would be worse than riding astride an Icelandic horse.

Once on our way, the preacher cleared his throat and said, "I am wondering where is Runi."

"He…" I found the words hard to say out loud. I started again. "He…"

The preacher looked at me sadly. "Lara, did he die?" I nodded and swallowed hard. He shook his head slowly from side to side. "The pox?" I nodded again. He sighed and said, "I also have sad news." I looked at him, dreading his words.

"The pox ran through our people like a wild fire. Nearly three-quarters of all our folks died. We have been through a time of tribulation and trial."

I put my hand on his arm, partly to comfort him and partly to steady myself. "Runa? Agnas?" I asked.

"Our dear Agnas died. I am so sorry. I helped Runa to nurse her as best I could, but then Runa also became ill. I do not know how I was spared."

Agnas gone. I would never see her dear face or hold her gnarled hands again. "Runa?" I asked again.

"Runa lives, but I must warn you. You may not recognize her. The pox left her terribly disfigured. And…" he hesitated. "And she is blind."

I felt the sky falling down on me and I nearly dropped from my seat. The preacher grabbed my arm. "Do not give in to despair. You are stronger than that, Lara. Runa needs you."

I shook my head and breathed deeply. Runa needs me. Ja. I will be strong for Runa.

When the wagon reached the top of the hill approaching Runa's hut, Raven came bounding toward us. He nearly went under the wagon wheel, so the preacher stopped and I got out. I knelt down and held the pup. He whimpered and pawed my shoulders. Poor Raven. He has also been through a lot. Dorthe climbed out. "If yonder is the hut, we can walk the rest of the way," she said.

"Ja. Takk for the ride. We leave again tomorrow morning," I told the preacher.

"I will take you back to Torshavn in the morning, then. There are few people to minister to here now," he said sadly and he drove on down to the church.

Dorthe listened sympathetically as I told her of the fate of Agnas and Runa. By the time we reached the hut, we were in agreement that Runa must go with us to Iceland.

The door opened just as I reached for the latch. "Who is it?" Runa asked.

The preacher was not exaggerating. Runa had the same unruly hair and clothing, but angry red scars marked her face and hands. Her eyelids were nearly scarred shut and even her lips were misshapen, so that spittle collected on one side.

"Runa," I began.

223

She immediately reached out for me and I held her. I had never thought that Runa could be so broken. She sobbed and clutched me so tightly, I could barely breathe. "Lara. You live." How could I not have thought that she may be worried about me as well? I continued to learn that I am not the only one who suffers from what might be. "Runi?" She reached out and touched Dorthe's arm.

Dorthe said, "I am Lara's fetter – fraendi – from Norway. My name is Dorthe."

Runa again asked, "Runi?"

I continued to hold her tightly and spoke in her ear. "Runi is gone, too, dear Runa. I am so sorry." She collapsed in my arms and Dorthe quickly reached over to help me get her into the hut where we laid her on her badsofa. I got a wet cloth for her head and Dorthe held her hand. Her eyes fluttered. "Was it the pox?"

"Ja."

"Did he suffer?"

"Everyone suffered," replied Dorthe.

CHAPTER 77

I went to the drying shed and discovered that the dried fish and meat were gone except for a few puny scraps. The root cellar was similarly bare. There was not enough food for a meal for the three of us. "How did you manage, Runa?" I asked.

She sat up and rubbed her arms. "A lad whose family died wanted to take over the fishing business, so in exchange for the boat, he agreed to bring me fresh fish and bread when he had it. I can still filet fish by feel. And Raven. Raven helped with the sheep and he helped guide me when I walked anywhere." Hearing his name, Raven went to Runa and rubbed against her leg. Runa petted his head and stood up. "I am not one to feel sorry for myself. I get along."

I thought about how hard everything would be without sight and was amazed that she was surviving. "Runa, we need to make a decision. I know this is abrupt, but Dorthe and I would like you to come with us. We are going to my home in Iceland. We have a ship already hired to take us tomorrow."

"Tomorrow? Leave my home? I do not know…." her voice trailed off, but I could see that she was thinking.

The preacher appeared at the door. "A basket of cheese and bread for you. I know there is not much at this hut." He held the basket out to me.

"Come in. We were just talking to Runa about coming to Iceland with us," I said.

Runa sat in Agnas' chair by the hearth, and the preacher sat in the rocking chair. He folded his arms and looked at Runa's ravaged face. "Um hum, um hum," he repeated as he rocked back and forth. Dorthe and I sat at the table and waited. I understood Runa's feelings. She had never lived anywhere else. The preacher had been good to her, but he was not a young man. I was afraid that, if she stayed, she would die. But I could not force her to go.

Dorthe jumped up. "We will think better with food in our bellies," she declared. She found a knife and sliced the bread and cheese. She took Runa's hand, turned it palm side up, and placed some food in it. Dorthe was a marvel to me. How did she know to do that? We all helped ourselves and chewed in silence.

"I will be right back." I took a small bucket outside and dipped fresh cold water from the spring. When I returned, it was as if the scene was frozen except for the chewing. We took turns drinking from the bucket. I looked around the room. The crèche that Runi carved was still on the shelf above the hearth, along with my carved angel. They were all covered with dust and soot.

I walked over and picked up the angel. "What are you doing?" asked Runa.

"I am looking at the carved angel. Do you remember it?" I asked.

"Of course I remember it. When Runi gave it to you, he said, 'an angel for my angel.' Can you find something to wrap it in? We will need to wrap the other figures and a few other things I will want to take with me."

I looked at Dorthe and the preacher. He nodded, "Um, hum," and Dorthe's eyebrows shot up. I looked at Runa and beheld a most beautiful sight. Runa smiled.

We spent the evening packing Runa's clothes, her tools, and a few things from Agnas: a blanket, a scarf, and one of her big spoons. Runa sat in Agnas' chair like a queen and directed the activities. She said that if she did not ask us to pack something, she wanted it left. That meant Runi's things, too. I took the bright blue cap that Agnas knitted for him for Christmas and tucked it in my pack. I liked to remember the way the color matched his eyes. The preacher gave church funds to Runa to buy the hut and sheep, planning to repay the church when the property sold. He promised to give St. Luke, the bellwether ram, a permanent home with him, since he was Agnas' favorite. All the hurried activity made the work feel exciting. We finished up and when he was ready to leave for the night, the preacher had a load of things in his basket that Runa wanted him to keep. I think it was easier for her to think that someone who she cared about had some of her things. The preacher called for St. Luke and I heard his bell clang more and more softly as the ram accompanied him down the hill to the church house.

Dorthe climbed into my old badsofa and I climbed into Runi's. When I closed the door, I buried my face in his blankets where a faint scent of him remained. I closed my eyes and tried to sleep, but Runi's scent aroused me so powerfully, I had to get up. I paced a while, got a drink of water, then crawled into Agnas' badsofa. I forgot to tell Runa that Dorthe and I were wearing trousers. I would have liked to see the look on her face if she could have seen us.

A loud knock on the door woke me with a start. Was it morning? Raven barked furiously and Dorthe and Runa were soon awake as well. I went to the door and, in the faint light of early dawn, saw the silhouette of a tall man. For a moment, in my sleepy stupor, I thought it was Runi and my heart jumped. Dorthe came behind me and said, "Arne. Why are you here?"

"I am sorry to startle you, but we have to ship out earlier than planned. A storm approaches. If we leave now, we can outrun it."

I gathered my wits and stepped outside, shutting Dorthe, Raven, and Runa in the hut. "Captain. There has been a change of plans here, too. We will have another passenger. Runa is going with us to Iceland. Oh. And a dog, Raven."

He smiled when I said 'a dog,' and replied, "We will work it out. Just please come quickly. I have a wagon waiting."

Dorthe and I hustled our packs onto the wagon and Arne helped with Runa's things. I quickly wrote a note to the preacher and Arne gently helped Runa into the wagon. Dorthe offered to ride in the back with Runa. When everything was loaded, I called, "Raven!"

She tried to jump onto the wagon, but the years had taken a toll on poor Raven. Arne jumped down, picked him up and gently placed him between Dorthe and Runa. Then Arne climbed onto the bench next to me. He handed me the reins. "I will relax now," he said.

CHAPTER 78
KIRKJUBOUR TO TORSHAVN FAROE ISLANDS TO AKUREYRI ICELAND

Arne leaned back and closed his eyes while I told him what I had learned about Agnas and Runa. He said that he would give Runa free passage to Iceland. "My wife died of the pox. What a terrible disease. If I can help a survivor, I will."

"Anna no doubt told you about my husband, Runi. If not for your soster, I do not know how I would have lived."

"We all must help each other. That is the way to a happy life," he said.

When we arrived at the harbor, Arne sprang into action. He had a boat waiting to take us out to the ship. We quickly loaded into the boat. Raven sat in the middle, his open mouth forming a happy smile. Arne removed his coat rowed expertly with taut arm muscles pulling on his shirt sleeves. Dorthe's eyes met mine and she lifted her eyebrows a few times.

At the ship, we trained Runa's hands onto the ladder and she climbed up like a seasoned sailor. The rest of us followed, Arne with the squirming Raven under his arm. As soon as Arne's feet hit the deck, he began to call out commands and sailors scurried to their posts. Without delay, we sailed on a stiff breeze out into the North Sea. I hoped that, in our haste, we did not leave anything that was important to Runa behind, and that the preacher would find my note.

The predicted storm did follow us for a day. We could see the dark shelf of clouds behind the ship, and it lent some powerful wind to speed our journey. The following days on the sea were quite placid, but there was enough wind to keep the sails working. I read aloud to Runa from the Bible. She liked the story of David and Goliath best, especially when I told her about Fadir's teachings with the sling. I told her all of the things I confided to Dorthe. She listened without reaction, but when I revealed that the shot from my sling resulted in Pjetur's death, she said, "Good." Raven, who sat at our feet, stood up and barked.

Each day, I told her a bit more of my story. She was a good listener; she never interrupted. When I finished, I asked, "Do you want to tell me about anything that happened while I was away?"

She was quiet so long, I thought she might have dozed off. It was hard to see if her eyes were open or shut. She put her finger to her lips and then folded her hands. " I bore a constant anger, like my fadir did. But when Modir became so ill and then I succumbed to the pox ... and you and Runi did not return, I fell into deep despair. My work and my family were my whole life. And then all of that was taken from me." She rubbed her arms and then touched her cheek. "Now I am ugly. I am blind." She smiled, "But I am no longer angry."

"Why?" I asked.

Runa shrugged, "Life is short. I do not have time for it anymore. Besides," she said, "I prayed and God brought you back to me. I am grateful." Her smile was like sunshine. Because I loved her, Runa was beautiful.

While Runa and I spent quiet time together talking and reading, Dorthe and Arne were together. Even when he was working, Dorthe sat quietly in his cabin, watching or reading. He dictated his ship's log entries to her, and she wrote them out in her careful hand. From time to time, I heard her playing the fiddle or her victory "whoop" when she won at the kings and queens game she played with him. If Raven were with them, he would follow up with a "woof." At night, the three of us crawled over each other to get into bed: I was by the wall, then Runa's cot was wedged in the middle, and Dorthe's by the door. The door would only open part way because it was such a tight squeeze. Sometimes Raven would want to sleep with us, and when he did, he would squeeze under the beds and snore beneath us. We treated every night like a party. While waiting to fall asleep, we told each other stories and sometimes Dorthe would bring ale or other spirits from the Captain for us to share. When Dorthe crept out in the night, I wondered if she was using the latrine or visiting Arne. I was done with spying and meddling in others' affairs, though, so I just rolled over, went back to sleep, and kept still about it.

Finally, one day at dusk, while standing on deck, I at first thought I saw a bank of clouds, but as the ship drew closer, I could see the mountains of Iceland. Rounding to the northern part of Iceland and entering the long fjord took all night; it was morning by the time we reached the harbor at Akureyri. Although it was summer, the morning air was cool. We gathered our packs and wore shawls against the wind. Thankfully, this was a deep port with a wharf, so the ship was tied up and the gangplank lowered. We did not have to climb down a rope ladder. Perhaps arriving in Iceland at a place where I had never been made it easier, or maybe having both Dorthe and now Runa with me helped, or I might have just adjusted to the idea, but my worries about returning home were less crippling now and I began to feel eager to see my friends and family again. We tidied up the cabin and left some coins for the second mate for letting us use his space. Dorthe said, "I am going to wait for Arne and see if I can help him. Meet you on the wharf?"

Leaving the ship, Runa did not want me to help her, she preferred to let Raven come alongside her leg and guide her. She was still Runa, after all. Independent and capable. I dressed in my best Icelandic clothes, but Runa wore her Faroese lads' garb, complete with her knife in her belt. I wondered what Modir, Fadir, and especially Ole would think of my friends.

We took an outdoor table at a tavern on the wharf and, thankfully, the sun came out to warm us up. A plump, exhausted looking barmaid approached us, "What will you have?"

"Do you serve coffee?" I asked

"Ja. We have hot coffee, milk, sugar."

"Takk. We will have two coffees."

Runa piped up, "And biscuits and butter, too. Oh, and some meat scraps and water for our friend."

"She means the dog," I said.

"Ja. I see the dog," the woman said, "I call my dog my friend, too." She patted Raven's head.

Just then, she noticed Runa's face. She looked at me with alarm. I shook my head at her and said, "We will surely enjoy our breakfast. Takk."

The barmaid understood that she was dismissed. She glanced at Runa once more and left. I wondered how Runa would be treated if she were not with someone else to intervene for her. We listened to the sounds of the ships being unloaded, the men calling orders to each other, the wagons being filled and the clop-clop of the horses as pulled their heavy loads. A man came out of the tavern and walked straight to me. "I would like a word with you, please," he said.

"Who are you?" I asked.

"I am the owner of this place. Please. Just over here." He motioned with his hand.

"I will be right back," I said to Runa.

The man spoke in a whisper, his back to Runa. "I am asking you to leave my place. That woman's face will scare away other customers."

I could feel the heat rise in my chest. "Leave? We just ordered food and drink." I looked him in the eyes. "She will not give her scars to anyone. She survived the pox. That is all."

He raised his voice, "I want you out."

Suddenly Runa and Raven were at my side, "What is the problem?" Runa flipped her knife over and over in her hand, like a magic trick. "If you do not have biscuits, bread is fine. But bring butter. I will use this to spread it." She touched the tip of the knife to her tongue.

The man backed away and when he reached the door, Runa called, "And do not forget the food for my friend."

The barmaid brought our coffee and food almost immediately. None of us spoke a word. Raven ate her meat scraps and drank water with noisy slurps. Runa and I began to eat and then I saw Dorthe waving as she skipped down the gangplank. She plopped down by us and took my coffee cup from my hand. "Mmmm... and biscuits, too? I am so hungry." She reached for a biscuit.

Runa said, "Let me butter that for you." I laughed.

Dorthe looked from me to Runa and back again. "What have you two been up to?"

I leaned in to tell her and just then, the barmaid appeared to ask Dorthe if she wanted anything.

"I will share the biscuits. A cup of coffee, please." Dorthe waved at Arne who was leaving the ship. "And another coffee for my ... friend. Maybe a few more biscuits, too."

"Another friend. Ja," she muttered as she walked away.

Arne pulled up a chair and scratched Raven under the chin. "I have secured a wagon to take us to your home, Lara."

"You are going, too? Wonderful," I said.

Arne replied, "I will not be able to stay long, but I will be sure you arrive safely." Dorthe beamed. I knew she was not ready to say goodbye to Arne. Two more cups and a plate of biscuits arrived.

"Ah, breakfast," Arne said. "I am so hungry." That is what Dorthe said, too.

CHAPTER 79
HOME ICELAND

We walked a short distance to a livery stable where a wagon with a driver and a sturdy Icelandic horse were waiting for us. Arne brought a map and I showed the driver where my home was. The driver scratched his bald head, "There are a lot of hills between here and there. Some of you may have to get out and walk."

We all agreed that we could walk if we needed to. The wagon was loaded. Arne sat up front with the driver and the rest of us piled into the wagon with the packs. I am not sure if Raven sensed my excitement or if I sensed his. He paced and climbed around on us and my breath came in quick bursts. As soon as we left the busy port at Akureyri, the countryside became a familiar blend of red and gray rocks, hills, rivulets, thatches of grass and shrubs. Cresting a small hill, we were all startled by a field of purple lupine. "How beautiful." Dorthe said.

"Tell me," said Runa. It was nearly impossible to describe what we saw, but Dorthe and I both tried. I also told them about Modir, Fadir, and Ole and my friends, Kristin, Edda, and the lads: Tryggve, Olav, and Birgir.

"Everybody out," called the driver. We walked behind the wagon up a steep hill and then got back in after we were at the bottom again. Raven wanted to run, but I kept him near us, since he did not know where we were going.

Soon some sheep crossed the path and I saw that their ears had the Arnesen's notch in them. I knew we were getting close. Then I saw the fine yellow house on the hill. "Look," I said, "The Master Arnesen's house."

Arne turned sharply and looked at me. "Did you say Arnesen?"

"Ja. It is the master's house. Soon you will be able to see my home. It is nearer the water."

"But Arnesen. That is my family name. I am Arne Arnesen, named after my far."

My heart skipped. What might that mean?

"I would like to visit that yellow house to see if they are my kin," Arne said. He turned to the driver. "I will get out there." The driver stopped and Arne jumped down. "That is your home?" he pointed to the hut. "I will join you there." He turned to the house.

"That is a surprise," said Dorthe. "But Lara. Your home. I want to run. Do you?"

"Runa, do you mind staying with the wagon? Raven will run with us."

"I will ride all the way to your home," Runa said.

Dorthe, Raven, and I jumped from the wagon and ran down the hill all the way to the hut. It looked smaller than I remembered, and the garden seemed forlorn. Raven chased the chickens that were pecking near the hut. Out of breath, I reached for the door latch and looked back at Dorthe. She laughed. "Go ahead. Open it." The familiar creak of the door, the smell of the hearth, and there at the table – my dear Modir. She saw me and fell to the floor.

I ran to her and held her as she shook and cried. We sat together on the floor crying and rocking together until I felt a tap on my shoulder. I turned to see a handsome little boy. "Lara?" he asked.

"Ole!" I grabbed him and pulled him onto my lap. "You remember me?"

"Maybe," he said. He pulled a silver pendant from inside his tunic. "Do you have one of these?"

I smiled and pulled out my pendant. He clinked his against mine. "A match," he said.

CHAPTER 80

Runa and the packs arrived and soon our little hut was crowded. I introduced Modir and Ole to Dorthe. Modir was happy to meet one of Fadir's kin. Runa reached out her hand and Modir took it between hers. "Welcome," she said.

"Modir, where is Fadir?" I asked.

Ole took Modir's hand. She shook her head, "Oh, Lara, I am so sorry to tell you he died of the pox last year." Did I know in my heart that he was gone? I think I may have. I wished I could talk to dear, wise Fadir again. I knew I would miss him terribly, but I had been afraid that my whole family had died. I still had Modir and Ole. I finally understood what Runa tried to tell me about life being short and being grateful. I just could not mourn any more. Dorthe took my hand and squeezed it. She knew. She had lost her far, too.

"Dorthe, do you want the pocket knife back. You meant it for my fadir."

"Give it to Ole. Your far would have liked that, and mine, too."

Modir said, "Please sit, everyone. I will boil water for tea." There were not enough chairs; Dorthe and Ole sat on the bed. His legs reached the floor. He would grow to be a tall lad. I asked about my friends. Modir said, "When you did not return with the others, Kristin gave us your gifts and told us what had happened. Birgir, who I have come to know, devised a story to tell to everyone else that Pjetur's horse showed up at the camp, but Pjetur did not. Birgir said that Pjetur must have emigrated, having got big ideas at the Thing. That is what everyone repeated. They said that maybe you ran away with him. Folks had a hard time believing that, but they were not given any other explanation. Finally it was accepted. I knew the truth, though, and I prayed every day that you would return after your exile. She smiled, "And here you are. My prayers were answered."

"What about Edda?" I asked.

"Ja. Well, Edda had a baby. She claimed that the boy was Pjetur's, and he did have the same weak eyes and spindly frame, but the Arnesens did not accept the baby as their kin. Edda continued to work in their kitchen and care for her baby until the pox." Modir sighed. "The pox took Edda and her baby. Herre and Fru Arnesen also died of the pox. Einar survived, but he is not well. He cannot breathe enough to walk even a stone's throw. Ashild, the old woman missing a hand, nurses him." Modir looked over at Runa and stood to prepare the tea. I found three cups. Ole and I did not have tea. There was no milk or sugar in the house so they sipped it plain. When she sat again, Modir continued. "Kristin and Birgir married. Her fadir also died; they are crofters in his place." That did not surprise me. They were a good match.

"Do you know about Tryggve or Olav?" I asked.

"The tall cousins. Ja. They both live. They work at the next farm." She paused. "Neither one is married. Not that you asked."

"I have things to return to each of them." I counted on my fingers as I recalled each one. "Kristin's Bible, Birgir's Vegvisir, Tryggve's fancy blade, and Olav's fishing net. I carried them with me the whole time." I looked at Ole, "And I have Fadir's sling and your Afi's pocketknife for you. We will teach you how to use them."

A knock at the door startled us. Dorthe jumped up to answer it. Raven ran inside the hut and sat by Runa. Arne removed his hat, ducked down to enter, and looked around. Modir stood, "Welcome. You are with Lara's group?"

"Modir, this is the captain of the ship that brought us here."

"I am Arne Arnesen. I have just come from the place you call the yellow house."

"Arnesen." Modir repeated, "Are you kin to Einar?"

"Ja. We just discovered that his far was my long-lost bror. I would have liked to see my bror again." Arne looked down at his hat. "Einar is not well. I will sell the estate to help pay for his care. The one-handed woman is also in need of care."

Dorthe said, "I have the money from selling my homestead. I have been thinking that by rights, part of that money should go to Lara's family, since it was her far's home, too."

"I have the money the preacher gave me for my place," Runa said.

"I think I can give you a good price," Arne said with a wink at Dorthe.

Dorthe clapped her hands. "Lara. I will give it to you. I will not be living here."

"Dorthe. What are you talking about?" I asked.

"Arne has asked me to marry him. I will have a life on the seas and with Anna in Bergen." She looked at Arne who was smiling like Raven does when she is happy. "Of course, you are to visit whenever you can."

My mind was in a swirl. I thought about all of the possibilities. We would move to the yellow house where Modir would have a big kitchen with milk and sugar and cups and chairs. Runa would stay with us. We would teach Ole to use a knife and a sling. Raven would help with the sheep and assist Runa. Perhaps Tryggve and Olav would come to work here for a share in the farm.

CHAPTER 81

When I next saw Hildur, she was standing at the cradle of Hans, who was just learning to sit up. He reached for her as she backed toward the door. Tugging her hat and twitching her whiskers she said, "I go before your husband returns. Tryggve does not believe in Huldufolk."

LIST OF CHARACTERS

ICELAND
Modir & Fadir: Lara's mother and father
Ole: Lara's little brother

Herre & Fru Arnesen: landowners where Lara's family works
Pjetur: one of the Arnesen twins who went to Thingvellir
Einar: one of the Arnesen twins who went to Thingvellir

Kristin: Lara's pious friend
Edda: Lara's orphan friend who consorts with Pjetur
Tryggve: Olav's cousin who went to Thingvellir
Olav: Tryggve's cousin who went to Thingvellir
Birgir: Olav and Tryggve's friend who went to Thingvellir
Raven: Tryggve's sheepdog

FAROE ISLANDS
Agnas: Runa & Runi's mother
Johan: Agnas' (mostly absent) husband
Runa: Agnas' daughter
Runi: Agnas' son
The Preacher

NORWAY

Anna: the Bergen innkeeper

Arne: Anna's brother, ship's captain

Bestemor and Bestefar: Lara's maternal grandparents

Sara and Knud: Lara's aunt (her mother's older sister) and uncle (Knud is Sara's husband)

Tollaf: Lara's uncle (her mother's brother) who lives in Trondheim

Hans: Lara's uncle (her mother's brother) who drowned

Lars: Lara's cousin who works at the ironworks, child of Sara and Knud

Johannes: Lara's cousin, child of Sara and Knud

Elizabeth: Lara's cousin, child of Sara and Knud

Dorthe: Lara's paternal cousin (Dorthe's father and Lara's father were brothers)